Alma Fritchley was born in 1954 in a small market town in Nottinghamshire, and has lived in the Manchester area for the last twenty years. *Chicken Run*, the first Letty Campbell mystery, was published by The Women's Press in 1997.

Also by Alma Fritchley from The Women's Press:

Chicken Run (1997)
Chicken Out (1999)

ALMA FRITCHLEY
CHICKEN FEED
A LETTY CAMPBELL MYSTERY

First published by The Women's Press Ltd, 1998
A member of the Namara Group
34 Great Sutton Street, London EC1V 0DX

Copyright © Alma Fritchley 1998

The right of Alma Fritchley to be identified as the author of this work
has been asserted by her in accordance with the Copyright, Designs
and Patents Act 1988.

British Library Cataloguing-in-Publication Data
A catalogue record for this book is available from the British Library.

ISBN 0 7043 4570 6

Typeset in Plantin 11/12pt by FSH Ltd, London
Printed and bound in Great Britain by Cox & Wyman Ltd,
Reading, Berkshire

This book is dedicated to Eileen

Acknowledgements

Thanks are owed to almost everyone I know, but especially to friends and colleagues in Stockport: Gail, for staying awake while I droned on; Julie, for her generosity of time and space. And thanks also to Pat, Carole and Brenda for their valuable word games and Fran for unravelling the knots. Mick, your patience held out; and Joss and Sue, your support has been extraordinary. Everyone else, just thanks.

Chapter 1

When I waved Anne off at the airport, I was convinced I'd never see her again. I blame the ancient Babylonians. Them and the International Women's Day celebrations held in San Francisco.

You wouldn't think these events would go hand in hand would you? Babylon, San Francisco and International Women's Day don't seem to have an obvious common theme. Anne, my lover, and her librarian cronies, however, would have no problem making the connection.

I'll explain, but briefly, lest I bore you.

Anne, sadly, was lost to the plight of the much-maligned Old Testament Babylonians. No matter how often she invited me to share this strange and fascinating era of history, somehow I couldn't drag myself away from *Brookside* to join her. Hard to believe that I'm in the minority here. When word got out that Anne had put pen to paper, or in this case microchip to word processor, and was actually writing about the subject, well, the phone never stopped. We had calls from the strangest places. Scribes from Saudi, Singapore and Southport wanted a piece of the action. Far from being a weird subculture, Anne's work had tapped into a vein that seemed to hold worldwide interest. It was, and still remains, a mystery to me.

Of our four-year relationship, I'd lost twelve months to a defunct tribe and a dead language. But it made Anne happy, and eventually marginally famous – enough, at any rate, for the female literati to invite her over to the States for countrywide lectures. That impressed me no end, except for several things. We had no idea where the lectures were to be held. I know that sounds crazy, but final arrangements were yet to be made. She would only know herself when she arrived in the States. Anne would be gone for three months and there was no way, no how, that I could go with her. I have a farm to run and even her eccentric niece, AnnaMaria, wouldn't agree to look after chickens for that length of time.

So two days before International Women's Day and Anne's first lecture, Manchester Airport was witness to a lesbian ritual as old as time itself. Tears, fears and promises were exchanged as other travellers pretended we didn't exist. With her own not insignificant work of non-fiction tucked under her arm, my soon-to-be-missed lover left me with a kiss and a final hug. My last impression of this handsome woman was the whoosh of her long coat against her woollen trousers as she hurried to the departure lounge.

The true pain of missing her would hit me later, but for now emptiness, like a peculiar hunger, filled the space between breast and stomach.

My attempts to quell the feeling by stuffing my face with overpriced airport junk food failed. Vegeburger and chips were not what I needed. The next flight out would probably have done the trick, but images of starving chickens left me guilt-ridden and AnnaMaria's disapproval would have haunted me all my days. I had no choice but to go home.

Calderton, West Yorkshire, home of my Little Farm on the Prairie, was a mere hour and a half away. A simple abode of pine walls and furniture, it was big enough for Anne, her niece and me to rattle around in comfortably.

There'd been several changes, though, since we began to live together. A librarian (with international links via the recently accessed Internet), Anne had changed dramatically with her growing interest in all things biblical. Women priests and vicars of different denominations and faiths had become frequent visitors after her theological articles had appeared in various publications. Anne had had many a late night with these women, the culmination of which (despite the unfortunate title) was the unexpected hit *Babylon, Then and Now.*

She took a six-month career break, bought the computer, tapped into the Internet (neither of which would be touched before her return) and pissed off abroad.

I knew I was bitter. I was also upset and lonely, and I was dreading getting home, knowing that's where I'd miss her most. The daily routine – the tap, tap of her typing, the grinding of the fax and the constantly ringing phone – while irritating, was part of her. But teatime, when everything was switched off, no matter what she was up to, was our time. In summer, tea in the garden, among the flowers and the clucking hens, maybe followed by a rare trip to the pictures in Leeds or a rarer foray to a club in Manchester. Winter saw us cuddled in front of a video, toasty beside the fire.

AnnaMaria was never in, ever. I sometimes thought she'd left home without telling us. Her work kept her busy, busier, busiest. A mechanic by trade, she'd sunk her savings into a car dealership with an old friend and ex-lover of mine, Julia.

Despite my reservations and Anne's unheeded warnings, AnnaMaria had taken the plunge and, amazingly, it had been successful in a small local way. Julia's big-time disasters of the past hadn't followed her to Calderton and the second-hand car business (mostly ex-company saloons or police vehicles fixed up by AnnaMaria and sold at a tidy profit by Julia) kept them both comfortably in pocket. They'd never make a fortune, but Julia had been down that road before and had been badly burnt. She was a bit too old and a bit too scared to compete with the big boys again.

So with everyone's absence accounted for, a dark and empty house beckoned. Or so I imagined.

Chapter 2

The farmhouse lights blazed across the hills, a beacon on the darkening skyline. For a moment they had me believing that Anne had chosen not to go to California and had come home instead. A strange caravanette of European origin parked on my driveway destroyed this idea.

I left the car, a loaner from Julia, at the front of the house.

'Letty,' a low voice hissed from the garden.

It was too dark to make out who was sat bundled up in a garden chair.

'Letty!' she hissed again, louder this time.

'Julia?' I asked, crunching my way across the drive towards her. The figure stirred and a match illuminated the features of my old friend. She drew deeply on a cigarette, the smoke drifting through the cold night air.

'Fucking hell, it's freezing,' she complained.

'Well, what are you doing out here? What are you doing here at all, come to that?' I demanded, gazing once more at my illuminated house.

'You don't have to be grateful,' Julia retorted, pulling a plaid car blanket tightly around her broad shoulders. 'But I thought you might be lonely.'

'You've not thrown a party?' I asked dreading the answer. It was just the sort of thing Julia would do unannounced.

'No, of course not,' she snapped, struggling out of the seat. 'And that's nothing to do with me either,' she went on, pointing to the odd vehicle. 'Ask AnnaMaria,' she added mysteriously, stamping her feet. The silk Paul Smith suit beneath the car blanket was doing nothing to keep her warm. 'Can we go in?' she moaned, shuffling off.

'Have I stopped you?' Exasperated, I followed her to the front door.

She turned to me on the doorstep, the light above the porch casting shadows over her troubled Italian features. 'Look, before you go in, I think I'd better warn you.'

The door opened before she could say any more.

An extra from *Oliver!* stared at me. Whisking thumb from mouth, the little urchin crushed me with a smile.

'Hello,' said I, warmed by the little girl's charm.

'Hello, Letty,' she lisped.

I looked at Julia, who shrugged her innocence.

'What's your name?' I asked the oddly dressed child.

'Wallis McNamara. I'm five and three-quarters. How d'ya do?' She stuck out her right hand for me to shake. Her tiny hand and sticky thumb were lost in mine during the very formal up-and-down greeting.

'Is your mum here?' I asked.

'She's dead," she said brightly. 'She lives on the moon now.'

I smiled but said nothing. I'm not one to contradict

children. It was hard to place her accent. Australian, New Zealand perhaps, maybe with a hint of something else.

A more familiar face and accent appeared around the corner of the door.

'Ah, Letty.'

'Ah, AnnaMaria,' I said equally brightly as Wallis McNamara and I stepped into the hallway.

The smell hit me then. 'What's that?' I asked, wrinkling my nose.

Wallis' tiny hand clutched mine again and she tugged for my attention. Dark corkscrew curls surrounded her pale face, dimples accompanying the angelic smile. She made Shirley Temple look like Hitler.

'Dock leaves,' she stated and dragged me down the hall towards my own kitchen.

'AnnaMaria,' I sang gently over my shoulder.

Dutifully she followed, a sick knowing expression on her face. Julia trailed behind, the car blanket discarded on the stair rail. Despite her protestations, Julia looked as guilty as the rest.

We struggled past a couple of bicycles that hadn't been there that morning and a worn-out rucksack that had nothing to do with me.

The stench of boiling leaves became stronger the nearer we got to the kitchen. Wallis' innocence aside, dread filled my every atom.

I was right to worry. A cauldron bubbled merrily on the Aga, the non-matching lid allowing a thick dollop of green liquid to hiss down the side of the hot metal. Steam filled the kitchen like a Turkish bath and a strange ethereal figure hovered near the sink. A dozen candles flickered in the half-light.

That was my first impression. A more realistic reaction followed closely. A total oddball with long curls obliterating all features was cooking something unmentionable on my stove.

I reached for the light switch.

'Don't,' a deep-throated but decidedly female voice commanded.

Startled, I withdrew my hand.

'Just give me a second,' the strange woman said more gently.

She clattered about at the sink doing things I couldn't guess at and after a moment took the pan from the hot plate. 'Okay,' she breathed quietly.

Julia beat me to the lights.

The woman looked in my direction. A long-fingered and beringed hand reached for her hair and she carefully brushed damp strands away from her mouth.

Julia, always one for a pretty face, and this one was gorgeous, almost swooned at my side.

A million questions clamoured for attention, but I could manage only, 'Do I know you?'

The woman smiled and the steamy atmosphere got steamier. Julia jabbed me painfully in the ribs. Shouldered aside, I watched my old friend switch to tart mode.

Before she could launch into her usual routine, the stranger got there first. 'Julia,' she stated.

'Yes,' Julia said, surprised. 'Do *I* know you?'

Wallis McNamara, having reached the boredom threshold of a five-year-old, hopped into the damp kitchen.

'Laura, Laura,' she sang, reaching for the woman's

hand and beating Julia to introductions. 'Can we go and see Gran now, please? Please?'

Laura bent to the little girl. 'Well, you help Julia and AnnaMaria to tidy the kitchen while I go and talk to Letty first, okay?'

'Okay,' Wallis agreed happily and she grabbed a dish cloth from the sink. 'Julia, you wipe round,' she ordered. 'AnnaMaria, you help me wash up.'

The two women had no choice but to obey. Laura, as in control as Wallis, beckoned me into the lounge.

Chapter 3

'Well?' I asked, sizing up the young woman.

Edging towards six feet tall, the fair-haired Laura had great presence. Mine was slipping by the second.

'Letty, you really don't know me at all, do you?' Her voice had the same twang as Wallis'.

'Should I?' I asked.

A crash from the kitchen accompanied my words.

'Sorry,' Julia's voice drifted in. 'I'll get you another.'

A pig flew past the window.

Laura draped her long-limbed body into a tall pine dining chair and took a moment to tie her hair into a loose ponytail with a colourful elastic band handily placed around her wrist.

The similarity and the answer to the mystery sledge-hammered me before Laura had a chance to explain herself.

'You're Anne's little sister, aren't you?'

She laughed and her face became Anne's. 'Not so little now.'

I sank into a chair opposite Laura.

'My God,' I managed. 'Where did you spring from? I know Anne's not heard from you for ages. Not since your mum died at any rate. What's that? Three years ago now?'

Laura reached into the breast pocket of her shirt and extracted tobacco and papers. 'Do you mind?' she asked.

I waved a stunned 'Go ahead'.

She rolled and lit a cigarette before replying. 'It's a bit complicated,' she admitted. 'Still painful too.' She scratched her forehead with her thumb. Wispy smoke drifted towards the ceiling as she reached once more into the cavernous shirt pocket and pulled out several photos. 'I've only recently learned the whole story myself.' She juggled with the pictures and her cigarette and looked around in vain for an ashtray.

'Get an ashtray for me, would you, Julia?' I bellowed.

'No need to shout,' Julia murmured from the doorway.

I looked around to find her carefully drying her hands on a tea towel. The silk jacket had been abandoned and the sleeves of her lilac shirt were carefully rolled to the elbows. I don't suppose Armani had had washing up in mind when he'd first designed the thing.

'Why don't you and AnnaMaria come in?' I offered. 'Laura was just telling me about her family.'

'No, it's all right,' Julia replied. 'We've just had a blow-by-blow account from Wallis. She's got a mean game of Monopoly lined up and she's looking forward to an opportunity to thrash me. She wants to play with real money too, though I don't suppose I could afford her terms. I'll get that ashtray.' She disappeared into the kitchen.

'It's not very often that Julia's charmed by children.

What do you put in Wallis' cocoa, for God's sake?'

Laura laughed as she passed me the photos. 'She's been on the road too long to be shy and retiring,' Laura confessed. 'The rest of it she inherited from her mother.'

'Who is her mother?' I asked, scanning the glossy pictures.

To my surprise my own face cropped up in a couple of them: Anne and I conked out on a Greek beach; Anne and her niece in a taverna. Wonderful holiday, wonderful memories from a couple of years ago.

'Anne sent them out after Mum's funeral. I couldn't afford the fare over then. That's Wallis' mum,' she continued, pointing to a hazy figure in climbing gear. 'She was my partner. She was killed in a climbing accident.'

'I'm sorry,' I said.

Laura shrugged. 'That's partly why I'm here, for Wallis' sake.' She paused as Julia delivered the ashtray. 'Thanks, Julia,' she said and slaughtered her with a grateful look.

Julia floated out of the room.

'But it's something I need to speak to Anne about really. No offence?' The smile was directed at me then and I could see Julia's point.

'None taken, but you've missed Anne. She's gone to the States.'

'I know,' Laura said, stubbing out her cig. 'AnnaMaria explained.'

I took a deep breath and plunged into troubled waters. 'Anne told me something about you. Your mother had you when she was quite a bit older, didn't she?'

I paused and Laura nodded for me to continue.

'She had you adopted,' I stated gently.

'Yes though the family thought I'd died at birth. Hard to imagine something like that happening now. She had reason enough, I suppose. Already with two grown-up children and then my dad dying while she was pregnant. All a bit of a tragedy really. I tried to trace Anne and Diane, my other sister, and found that Anne was the sole survivor. It took me ages and then I had to find the money to get here.' She laughed unexpectedly. "It's been a hell of a couple of years. And then to miss her by a day, damnit.'

'What will you do?' I asked innocently. I should have been prepared for the answer.

'Well, I was wondering if we could stay here for a while. There's just the three of us, me, Wallis and her gran. She's not very well at the moment.'

'Oh? What's wrong with her?' I asked.

She rolled another cigarette before replying. 'We had a bit of a run-in with the cops in Sydney.'

I waited for her to continue but her answer, when it came, was vague at best.

'We were involved with Greenpeace over there. You know how it is. We have a basic sort of lifestyle anyway and Gran isn't as young as she was.' She lit her cigarette. 'We wanted to come to England together,' she continued, avoiding further explanation. 'We'd stay in the van, of course. I was thinking maybe in one of your fields?'

Wallis came tearing into the lounge then and effectively made up my mind for me.

'I won,' she crowed, clutching a bag of pennies. 'AnnaMaria said it was the fastest game she'd ever

13

played.' She crawled uninvited onto my knee and carefully began to count her hard-earned cash.

'Of course you can,' I said to Laura. 'Stay as long as you want.'

Chapter 4

'Are you completely mad?' Julia demanded from the bedroom.

I spat toothpaste into the sink and wiped my mouth before answering. 'No,' I said as coolly as possible. 'What would you suggest?'

I switched off the bathroom light and got into bed. Julia was perched happily on the edge. No, we weren't having an affair; we were having an argument.

'Go to bed,' I ordered.

'Don't be tetchy,' she said. 'Just because you're having second thoughts.'

I punched the pillow into a comfortable position. It saved me punching Julia. I hated it when she was right.

She folded strong, tanned arms across her ample bosom. 'She could be anybody,' she stated loudly.

'Keep it down,' I hissed. 'You'll wake Wallis. I've already sung her every lullaby I know.'

'And Oasis' greatest hits!' Julia chortled. Provocatively she started to hum their latest million-seller.

I laughed aloud.

'Shh, you'll wake the baby,' she teased.

'Well, I couldn't let her sleep in that van, could I? It's freezing out there. The forecast said to expect unseasonably cold weather. It might even snow.' I was feeling righteous.

'According to Laura, they've been on the road for ages. They must have managed before. You saw that van – state of the art.' Julia sniffed. 'Anyway, how do you know she's who she says she is?'

'Julia, you've only got to look at her face. Cut her hair, add a few years and you'd be looking at Anne. You saw the photos.'

Julia blew disparagingly through her lips.

'They're not doing any harm out there,' I explained, more to myself.

'I bet you don't feel like that in three months. And that other woman, that Gran person. She was weird enough, and then when she drank that crap Laura had prepared for her, well, I nearly threw up!'

'She's a healer,' I slowly explained to Julia.

'Yeah, right.'

Typically, she was dismissive of anything that smacked of New Age ideology. The fact that healing herbs had been used since the human race first dragged itself around by the hair cut no ice with Julia. If it wasn't in a bottle with 'Take one four times a day after meals' written on it, it wasn't worth having.

'Gran *is* ill,' I insisted, pointlessly.

'I'm not surprised.' Rarely sarcastic, Julia was deadly when she put it to the test.

'You can't help your relatives. Look at yours!' I cackled.

'I've told you,' Julia replied frostily. 'The Mafia connection is just a racist rumour.'

It was my turn to blow a raspberry. After all, I'd met most of Julia's family and, while likeable people, there'd been more than an echo of *The Godfather*.

'What exactly are you going to do with them until Anne comes home?'

'Oh, I don't know. I've got some bushes that need trimming and the greenhouse needs a good sort-out.'

'I hope you've got third-party insurance. I don't think Gran could take much hard work. You can have my BUPA number if you like.'

'Piss off, Julia!' I growled. 'And go to bed. We'll talk in the morning. I've got to get up at six.'

'Oh, the joys of chicken farming. If I don't hear you snore in your sleep I may even help you.'

The airborne pig made another run past the window.

'Julia,' I said, exasperated, 'I'd have to see it to believe it.' I slid down the bed. 'Night, Julia.'

'Night-night, Letty.' Julia finally got up to go to the spare room. 'And don't worry about Anne. She'll be home before you know it.'

Five minutes later (or so it seemed), the alarm went off. A cacophony of cockerels outside my window had my adrenalin pumping. I pushed Jodie Foster away and groped for wakefulness. A sharp elbow was wedged into the small of my back. I'd had a nocturnal visitor and Wallis' black curls covered my pillow.

I struggled out of bed and Wallis stretched further. Dark brown eyes met mine and a smile crept to her face.

'Letty,' she squeaked and followed me out of bed.

I was tempted to give her the keys to the feed cupboard and climb back under the duvet myself, but I resisted and followed the lively child into the bathroom.

She sat on the toilet, singing Oasis songs, as I had a quick shower.

Finally I could talk. 'Come on, Wallis, let's get you washed.'

'I can wash myself,' she insisted and, stripping out of her too-tight nightie jumped into the shower.

She was even quicker than me. I threw her a towel and went in search of the rags she'd arrived in. There was no danger of her getting cold. The Aga kept the house warm and the background central heating had already kicked in.

I found her vest, knickers, one sock and an overall thing that may once have been a dress. Jeans and woolly jumper did me. The promised snow had arrived and I really didn't care what I looked like. I doubt if the chickens did either.

Wallis broke the world record at dressing. I found an old pair of socks that came to her knees, but she was blissfully unaware of her appearance. It was too early to consider why I was doing all this myself in the first place. Perhaps long-hidden maternal instincts were scrabbling for attention. It didn't bear thinking about.

'Do you want some breakfast?' I asked as we trundled downstairs.

'No, let's feed the chickens first,' Wallis insisted.

AnnaMaria had given her an account of the running of the farm. Feeding chickens, collecting their eggs and sweeping the yard held untold appeal to a five-year-old. Especially in the snow.

Fortunately I found both her wellies. My spare work boots would have been neither use nor ornament.

Her coat, like her nightie, was too small but would have to do. I found a woolly hat for her to wear and mittens she already had. Prepared at last, we ventured into the cold.

A light scattering of snow had fallen overnight and flurries threatened still. Wallis squealed with delight and pelted everything that moved with snowballs. I didn't mind, and even threw a few back, but the chicks weren't impressed. It's hard to imagine them as haughty creatures. She treated the eggs like, well, eggs really, and she was wide-eyed with wonder when a still-hot one was placed in the collecting tray.

I got a five-year-old's questions: 'Where do they come from?' 'How do they get there?' and, rather more difficult, 'Why do we eat them?' Did Laura tell her nothing?

I did my best, but my answers were always going to be unsatisfactory. She chatted brightly to Erik, chief cockerel, who was unsure of the correct reaction. He discovered, not for the first time, that all answers lay in his feedtray.

It was pointless sweeping the yard and I wondered if the two women in the van were all right. But as Julia had pointed out, their mobile home wanted for nothing.

Wallis' knees had gone an alarming shade of red, so we retreated to the warmth of the kitchen, where Anna-Maria and Julia were up and about.

Julia looked as though she was on her way to a job interview. I suppose for the best part of a thousand pounds you get a suit that holds its shape in whatever circumstances. The lilac shirt had been washed and dried overnight. It looked as though it had just been delivered from the laundry.

A modestly successful forty-something designer dyke, Julia was everything a woman could want and yet, as she was prone to misquote, 'Without the chase, I'm nothing.' Only once had I seen her lose her heart. A Scandinavian woman in the same line of business had loved and left her within the year and Julia still wasn't over it. I'd been fond of Julia for a long time, more so now than when we were lovers. She was far less complicated as a friend.

AnnaMaria, straight, uninterested in children – hell, she wasn't even interested in her boyfriend, Andy – was on her hands and knees on the kitchen floor doing the horse routine to Wallis' jockey. Had someone put something in the water? Maybe we were all having an early menopause and this was a last desperate attempt by our bodies to prolong the human race. But Wallis was cute, endearing and frighteningly intelligent, which was more than could be said for the rest of the household. Hardly surprising we'd all taken a shine to her, she was such a novelty.

'Listen, I've got to go,' Julia said through a mouthful of toast. 'I've got an appointment at the bank this morning.'

'Which one?' AnnaMaria asked suspiciously from the floor. 'You're not going into Manchester, are you? I'll never see you again today if you do.'

'No, don't panic,' Julia replied, shouldering her way into her jacket. 'I won't be long.'

'And you're going home tonight?' I asked, not relishing the thought of another evening with her.

'Yes, O ungrateful one. I shall retire to my little flat in

the big city. The house is all yours. I prefer my futon anyway,' she added with a sniff.

'I'm not surprised you don't trap off, sleeping on that thing,' AnnaMaria piped up. 'It's a wonder you don't get a hernia.'

'It never bothered the Japanese,' Julia replied, wagging a warning finger.

'They don't normally weigh twelve stone,' AnnaMaria observed drily.

'Now, now,' I interrupted. 'The day's hardly begun and you're already at each other's throats. How you two can work together is beyond me.'

Their garage was on the outskirts of Calderton, just off the A road to Leeds. Traffic was brisk enough for them to pull in trade and word of mouth had soon got around.

'Right, I'm off,' Julia said and, glancing in the mirror above the kitchen sink, finger-brushed her dark mane of hair. Light from the window picked out the odd bit of grey, but distinguished is a word that fits well with Julia anyway. 'I'll see you before I head home,' she promised me. 'And, AnnaMaria, don't be late,' she warned her still earth-bound colleague.

AnnaMaria ignored her. Instead she hauled Wallis to her feet and plonked her in front of a bowl of porridge, which the child ate without tasting. Probably just as well, as Julia had made it.

'Can I leave the table and play outside?' Wallis asked politely.

I had to steady myself against the sink. Good humour and good manners at seven-thirty in the morning were almost unknown.

'Yes, just wait till I wash up and then we'll go and see

Laura and Gran.'

Wallis whooped with delight and, grabbing her coat, shot out through the back door. Erik shrieked in terror and a bundle of feathers streaked across the slowly melting snow, away from Wallis' cold artillery.

AnnaMaria decided to walk to work. Her Kawasaki 650 refused to start and she figured a three-mile trek across icy fields wasn't such a big deal. Even if, like her, I was twenty-one again, the chances of me walking to work were pretty slim. Still, she enjoyed her work, whereas my previous job as an insurance clerk had never had my pulse racing. I thanked the Great Lord Bountiful once again that my old aunt had had the good sense to leave Calderton Brook Farm to me and not some waste-of-space cousin. She had also left me enough money to live on, of course. One was no good without the other.

Wallis finally came in from the cold and, after a warming cup of tea, we both piled into Julia's rental car, which she'd lent me for running Anne to the airport (my Land-Rover was awaiting repairs at AnnaMaria's garage and because I got family discount it meant mine was always left to last). A sudden pang had me longing for Anne. But if nothing else, the previous night's excitement made sure I didn't dwell on my recent loss.

The rental car, a ten-year-old Volkswagen Golf, started first time and little Wallis helped me clean the windows. The sky was clearing and the snow clouds were beginning to drift off, ready to cause mischief over the North Sea. Spring seemed to have finally turned a corner, the snow being winter's last gasp.

Chapter 5

I wasn't so much surprised when I found the field empty; horrified would be nearer. It didn't matter how much I scanned the horizon, the van had gone.

Long gone too, by the look of it. The last sprinkling of snow was free of any tracks except my own. Wallis seemed surprisingly unconcerned and instead fiddled with the CD player. I toyed with the idea that the two women had gone to the village. It was a possibility and one I clung to. The alternatives were too horrendous.

Wallis didn't help. 'They've done it before,' she said matter of factly during the short, panicky drive home.

'What?' I asked and turned the CD down before Jarvis Cocker burst my eardrums.

'Laura and Gran.' She paused and wiped the windscreen free of steam. 'They left me months and months and months once when I was really little.'

'Oh, God.' I groaned aloud. But what did months and months and months mean to a five-year-old? 'Can you remember where you were?' I asked carefully.

She gave me a disdainful look worthy of Bette Davis in *Hush . . . Hush, Sweet Charlotte*. 'It was in Australia, of course.' A few years older and she would have added, 'What a stupid question.'

'And what happened?'

'Oh, they came back. They bought me a new frock,' she added obscurely.

'Who looked after you?' I pressed, carefully avoiding pot-holes in the road.

'I don't remember,' she said. 'They had kangaroos.'

Defeated, I drove the rest of the way in silence, except for Jarvis of course.

The house was empty, the village was deserted, my phone was dead and I was getting a headache. Gran and Laura had gone. It was no good pretending otherwise. If they'd sneaked off in the night taking Wallis with them, well, that would have made them no more than a bit strange, but this was desertion.

I tried the phone again a couple of times but the sudden snow seemed to have played havoc with the lines. This was a regular occurrence but even so I'd never been tempted to get a mobile phone. Being cut off from civilisation wasn't such a bad idea some days, though today wasn't one of them.

The deserted village hadn't been such a shock, Aliens hadn't landed and made off with Calderton's inhabitants, it was just half-day closing. Contrary to the rest of the planet, Calderton opened late, rather than closed early one day of the week. Mrs Buckham, the cornershop proprietor, had tried to explain the reasoning behind it once, but an alderman in the nineteenth century and his quirky ways held no interest for me. The library and the post office as well as the corner shop were all shut up tight. Even the police station, an establishment I felt I would be visiting before too long, was closed till twelve.

My major problem, I realised on the final leg home, was Wallis, and she was a problem I wasn't prepared to deal with alone. Oh, God, where was Anne when I needed her? Three thousand miles away, that's where. Julia, though a poor substitute, would have to do. I let Wallis play in the yard as in desperation I scoured the house for a note, for some sign of responsibility, but there was no post, no note, nothing.

Wallis wandered back into the house. The chicks had gone into hiding (who could blame them?) and she needed feeding, entertaining but mostly cleaning. She needed a carer, in fact, and for the moment I was it.

I discovered that looking after chickens and looking after children weren't so different after all. You could chat to both of them and not get much sense out of either. A bath for Wallis was a case in point. She was muddy, smelly and damp. A promised cup of tea, which seemed to be the only thing she'd drink, and several chocolate biscuits later and she was putty in my hands.

With her skinny body surrounded by bubbles and curly hair cascading around her shiny face, Wallis gave me an enthusiastic account of her life so far. It was difficult to decide what was true and what was a product of her vivid imagination. Dragons in Tasmania were the final straw and I let her blabber on uninterrupted while I washed her hair. I didn't relish combing the dark locks though. Memories of childhood struggles between Mum and my hair ensured that these days mine was short and maintenance-free, but Wallis strode through the ill-treatment without a murmur. She even pointed out a bit that I'd missed with the cheap plastic comb. Finally, pink and smelling sweetly, Wallis emerged from the bath.

The problem of clothes (one small difference with chickens) was solved by an absent Anne. She'd taken to collecting jumble for some event that had never materialised, so somewhere in our vast attic were several bags of assorted clothes which, with a bit of luck, would hold something suitable. Wallis simply couldn't wear her old rags again.

There was something wrong with all this, I thought, as I carried a betowelled Wallis downstairs and plonked her in front of the telly (Richard and Judy could entertain her for a while) while I did the hunt and fetch routine. Laura had told me they'd had to scrape the money together to get here and their clothes reflected that, but the mobile home was worth easily fifteen grand. It was only a couple of years old, the fittings were new and state of the art. Perhaps they'd pinched it. Anything was possible. Christ, if you could dump a kid on a virtual stranger, what was a bit of thieving?

I dragged an ageing stepladder into position under the attic door and watched dust swirl around me as I forced the latch open. It was a place I rarely ventured into, such is my head for heights. By some miracle the long-unused electric light still worked. The hundred-watt beam dispersed shadows and spiders alike. I wasn't keen on either. My Aunt Cynthia, indulging in her love of pine, had not only walled the entire house with the softwood but similarly kitted out the attic. It was warm, dry and, apart from some of Anne's books and a few bin bags in a corner, empty. Mind wandering, I briefly contemplated the chances of turning it into a fourth bedroom, but soon realised that Julia would take it as her God-given right to adopt it as her home in the country. Anne would divorce me.

I retrieved the bin bags and pitched them down the stairs. Wallis could have some fun picking her own clothes.

Richard and Judy had been replaced by click click, beep beep. The joys of morning television cast aside, Wallis was now firmly plugged into the PC. Technically speaking, by comparison I was Stone Age woman, making fires with sticks and running away from thunder. She was blind to my presence and I watched over her shoulder, awed by her ability to know one end of the machine from the other. As far as I was concerned, that made her a child prodigy. Information scrolled across the screen and she yelled with pleasure when something caught her eye. I'd been happy with *Bugs Bunny* when I was her age.

I tapped her on the shoulder and her eyes were sparkling when she finally gave me her attention.

'You're not to play on that,' I said for want of something better. 'It's Anne's,' I continued, as though that explained everything.

Wallis exited from the machine without a grumble and switched it off. I didn't even know how to switch it on! I made a mental note to get her to program the video.

'Is she your girlfriend?' she asked, delving into one of the bin bags.

'Yes,' I replied, 'but she's in America now.'

'Is she coming back?' Clothes were being scattered across the floor.

I laughed. 'She'd better.'

'Do you love her?' A pair of jeans was examined and discarded.

'Yes, I do.'

'My mum used to love Laura,' Wallis stated, happily rooting around. A shirt met with her approval and she wasted no time in pulling it on.

'Do you know your dad?' I ventured, watching helplessly as my lounge disappeared under a sea of clothes.

'No. Mum said he was just a sperm.' I choked back a laugh. She was quite serious.

'Right,' I said noncommittally. 'What about these?' A miniature pair of Levi's seemed to leap into my hands.

'Ooh,' Wallis crowed, and I steadied her as she struggled first into her fading but newly washed knickers and then into the jeans. The Levi's had a hole in one knee and they were a bit baggy round the backside, but Wallis' look said they were a perfect, perfect fit. I even found a balled-up pair of socks with Dennis the Menace adorning the ankle. She looked positively trendy, though the wellies would have to go.

What was I thinking? What was I doing? I should have been banging on the police-station door by now, demanding some sort of action. Yet somehow there didn't seem to be much urgency. Wallis was quite happy and was convinced Laura and Gran would be back –

'Though probably not for ages and ages yet,' she'd said.

I had some sort of duty to inform the powers that be, but for the moment dressing her was a priority. We found another couple of outfits, both jeans-based, which I hung on the Aga to air.

We were dressed and ready to roll when a firm bang on the door and a rattle of the doorknob nearly had me diving for cover. There was only one person who could announce herself in such a forceful manner: Marks and Spencer woman, my mother.

I had thought she was on holiday. She was always on holiday, it was her reason for living. After twenty-five years as a solicitor's personal secretary, my mother knew how to play the system. You could be forgiven for thinking she'd taken early retirement, so little time did she spend in the office.

Her colleagues afforded her the deference she thought she deserved, especially her boss, Colonel Thompson. He looked exactly as he sounded: ex-Guards, public school, neatly clipped moustache, straight-backed and in his early sixties. My mother ran the poor man ragged. In an effort to keep her sweet and malleable, he bought her little treats: a brace of pheasant at Christmas after the Daybrooke Estate shoot, for example. I'm a vegetarian, so you can imagine how that went down. Choice cuts of venison from his estate in Scotland were another old favourite. He thought the way to his secretary's shorthand was through her stomach. A hundred-pound gift voucher from M&S would have done just as well. Probably less bloody too.

Her visit would solve one immediate problem though.

The concept of 'incommunicado' was alien to my mother. A gadget queen, she possessed not only a cellular phone but a car phone and a mobile fax, for God's sake. It had been especially imported from Japan by the Colonel in a vain attempt to keep tabs on her. Like the venison, another pointless and expensive exercise.

I caught a glimpse of her new car through the kitchen window. A raven-black 301E-series BMW with tinted windows and automatic sunroof. And she wondered why the police kept pulling her up! I didn't know where her money came from. Personally, I found her Tessa explanations a bit hard to swallow. Julia had been close to tears when Mum had first turned up with it unannounced six months earlier. Memories of beautiful cars she'd once owned and lost were more than she could bear. Her Ford Mondeo (part-owned with AnnaMaria) paled in comparison.

The doorknob rattled again.

'Letitia, Letitia, are you in?' Mum bellowed.

God, that name. Despite my objections (and since Aunt Cynthia's demise), only she used it in its Victorian entirety.

Wallis hid behind my legs. Even the chickens had retreated to their coop. It was too late to hide. She knew I was in. She could probably smell me sweating through the door. I threw the bolt and stepped back.

'Why on earth do you lock the door?' she demanded as she breezed in. Sleek grey hair expertly bobbed, she was the woman I would never be. Her dark blue double-breasted jacket and matching skirt jarred with my chicken farmer's outfit. Only our shoes shared a common heritage. She'd impressed on me as a child the importance of comfortable footwear. High heels would never make it to her feet as long as she drew breath. No surprise, then, when her first comment about Wallis concerned the child's feet.

'Those boots are too small,' she stated.

I was compelled to indulge her.

'It's all she's got,' I replied.

She tutted as only my mother can tut. Wallis emerged from behind my legs, though her thumb had disappeared into her mouth. Mum dumped her sensible handbag on the table.

'Then we'll get her some,' she said brusquely.

This attitude came with her job. The accent was pure Cheshire. Years of living in Macclesfield and careful cultivation had first diluted, then crushed her working-class Manchester accent. Mine was a mongrelisation of several regions. There was something of the sponge about me.

Mum pulled a pine chair away from the table and made a meaningful glance towards the kettle. I ignored the hint. She crossed black-stockinged legs (healthier than tights she would explain to anyone prepared to listen) and finally showed an interest in Wallis other than as a chiropodist.

'And who are you, dear?' she asked, kindly enough.

Wallis looked at me for some sign. I put the kettle on. That signal seemed to suffice.

'Wallis McNamara. How d'ya do?'

Her greeting was becoming familiar. Mum and Wallis solemnly shook hands.

'Are you a friend of my daughter?' Mum asked.

'Who's your daughter?' Wallis countered.

A slight frown flickered across my mother's remarkably unlined face. She'd finally met her match in the shape of a five-year-old.

'Letitia's my daughter, dear,' she said, pointing at me.

Wallis examined us both for a moment. 'She doesn't look like you.'

Mum managed a tight smile. 'Do you look like your mummy?'

'I don't know. She's dead.'

Mum's smile faltered. She looked to me for help – a first. I turned my back and made tea.

Eventually she had to ask. 'Letitia?'

'Mum, it's a bit – '

She held up her hand. 'Margaret, please.' The old hypocrite had hit a 'certain age' some years ago and 'Mum' was no longer in her vocabulary.

'Margaret, then. Look, it's a bit complicated.'

She raised a plucked eyebrow, whether in response to my reply or Wallis clambering onto her knee I would never know.

'Just lend me your phone, would you? The lines are down and I've got to ring Julia. I'll explain in a minute.'

The phone was produced.

'And how is Julia?'

Mum had never forgiven me for letting Julia slip through my fingers. Her assurance, connections and business acumen were something she felt I should aspire to, even if they had to come via a lover. She liked Anne well enough, though she felt Anne lacked Julia's sophistication. Librarian and writer were non-professions to Mum. She lives on another planet sometimes.

'Julia's fine. She stayed here last night.' I knew immediately that I'd said the wrong thing. The eyebrow was disappearing into her hairline as I dialled Julia's mobile number. 'She was just keeping me company, that's all.'

'Oh, of course. Anne's gone to America,' Mum said thoughtfully.

Wallis, now completely at ease, joined in the conversation. 'She's coming back though. She loves Letty, you see.'

Mum looked uncomfortable – another first. She was of the 'don't ram it down my throat' school of thought, or at least when it suited. Occasionally there was a certain amount of kudos to be had in having a dyke for a daughter.

The phone rang twice before Julia answered.

'Hello.' Voice, cool and sexy over the racket in the background. I knew at once she was on the road.

'Julia where are you?"

'Letty, darling, I'm on my way to the garage. Why, what's wrong?'

'Well, Mum's here.'

Julia laughed. 'Do you need rescuing?'

Julia could never understand why I had problems with my mother. They had always got on well.

'Sort of. Laura and Gran have gone.'

'Get out of the way, you fucking idiot!' Julia shrieked. A car horn sounded and more choice words were uttered to some poor, unsuspecting road user. Probably a lollipop lady, knowing Julia. 'Gone? What do you mean, gone?'

'I mean they've gone, left, deserted us, me and Wallis.

33

No explanation, nothing.'

There was a long pause.

'Julia . . .'

She cleared her throat. Guilt oozed over the line. 'Well, actually, I may be able to help.' Another pause. 'There was a letter for you behind the front door this morning. I picked it up and must have put it in my pocket. I forgot all about it. I've got it right here. It might not be from them,' she blundered on, 'but there's no stamp on the envelope.'

I seethed quietly. 'Can you bring it here, please? Now?'

'I'm just off to the newsagent's. Do you – '

'Now, Julia.' I broke the connection.

Mum took one look at my face and decided not to ask. Instead she turned fifty-odd years of accumulated charm onto an unsuspecting Wallis. But Wallis was impressed only when the mobile fax was produced. An immediate emotional link was forged by microchip.

The kettle had barely cooled when Julia roared into the yard. Her face was a portrait of envy when she espied Mum's BMW and a traitorous hand caressed its shiny damp hood.

Julia's face expressed quite another emotion when she let herself into the kitchen. She was fuming. I held out my hand for the expected letter.

'What's wrong?' I asked, aggrieved that she should think she had reason to be angry.

'Read this,' she ordered and slapped the local paper into my waiting hand. The letter was slung onto the kitchen table.

'Third column, page two,' she directed and dropped

heavily into a chair.

We were alone in the kitchen. Mum and Wallis had retreated to the lounge and Wallis was trouncing her opponent at *Killer Zombies II* on Anne's Sega system.

I shuffled through the *Calderton Echo*.

'MIDDLETON ROAD BYPASS. NEW PLANS TO GET GO-AHEAD?' it screamed.

'So?' I asked, puzzled. I couldn't see the problem.

'Letty!' Julia was clearly exasperated. 'What road is my garage on?'

'Batley Close. Why?'

'Which leads off where?'

'Oh, shit,' I said, realisation dawning. 'Middleton Road. But how come it's the first we've heard of it?'

Julia shrugged. 'I've no idea. But I'll find out. There's a meeting on at the Free Trade Hall tomorrow. That new Labour woman will be there to answer questions. Perhaps she'll be able to tell us something. Anyway, here's your letter.' Julia, despondent and completely uninterested in my problems, pushed the envelope across the polished surface. Definitely selfish at times, that one.

The envelope was unstamped and read simply 'LETTY AND WALLIS'. It didn't take a genius to know who'd written it. It started with an apology and ended with fighting talk.

Dear Letty and darling Wallis

I'm so sorry to have left you in the lurch like this, but we've just heard about the proposed bypass and we need to rally support fast. Letty, I know this is an imposition, but if you could just look after Wallis for a

few days . . . We'll be back with the others as soon as we can. This bypass can't go ahead. Have you any idea what effect it will have on the countryside? It's vital we stop it. See you in a few days.
Laura

'Oh, fuck it,' I muttered and shoved the note into Julia's hand. 'Are you familiar with the word "coincidence"?'

Her face lit up as she read it, but my expression stopped her getting too excited.

'What's the matter?' she asked. 'They'll be back soon.'

'Yes, but who with? Who are the others she's going on about? And where exactly will they be staying?'

My life had been disrupted enough already and Anne had only been gone one day.

Julia, trying unsuccessfully to keep a check on her emotions, made a bid for the common-sense approach. As usual, it only made things worse.

'Well, you've seen these people on the telly. They're all Greenpeace types. Save the whale. Drink more tea. Health through massage. That sort of thing.'

'Yes, I know what they're like,' I snapped. At the mention of tea, I reached for the kettle. When all else fails, make a brew. 'And what good do they do?' I pressed on. 'I mean, how many campaigns have they won, for God's sake? I can only think of one and that was down to a rare frog. I wouldn't rely on them too much, Julia. You may be sadly disappointed.'

'Don't be such a defeatist,' Julia scoffed, resting her size 6s on the table. 'All I want to know is why we've only just heard about all this. No one in the village has mentioned it. My God,' she said suddenly, 'what if there's a compulsory purchase order out on the garage. AnnaMaria would only blame me.' Julia went pale at the thought. If there was ever a problem with the garage, somehow it was always Julia's fault.

'Stop flapping, Julia. God, you're an emotional yo-yo today. And take your feet off the table. In fact, why don't you make us all a fresh pot while I have a word with Wallis. You can explain to Mum what's going on. It's nearly killing her.'

Julia's expressive face lit up. To say that she had a soft spot for my mother would be a major understatement.

Wallis took the news pretty much as I'd hoped. 'I knew she'd come back,' she said in a matter-of-fact voice. Perhaps Laura wasn't such a rogue after all. I would reserve judgement.

Another small problem pricked at the back of my mind and this one Wallis couldn't help me with. Julia, however, resolved it easily enough.

'Men? You think she'll bring men here?' she asked incredulously. 'Get real, Letty. We talked to her half the night. Don't you remember what she said? She can't abide them. I thought separatists had died off long ago, but they're still breeding them somewhere and Laura's the leader of the pack.'

Even mum raised a small laugh at that.

'Well, it was just a worry, that's all. I can't be doing with these New Man types at the moment.'

'You were never that keen on the old type,' Julia remarked drily. 'Anyway, while you're wittering, time moves on. I want to go to town and I need to change.'

Julia looked pristine, so there was no earthly reason why a new outfit was necessary, but I knew better than to question her about her wardrobe.

'Why?' I asked.

'Why what?' Julia replied.

I sighed. 'Why are you going to town? Shouldn't you be back at the garage?'

Julia cleared her throat nervously. 'I thought I'd take us all out for lunch.'

It took a moment for that to sink in. I hoped the moths in her wallet were prepared for the shock.

'I think that's a wonderful idea,' Mum declared. 'We all need cheering up.' Only Mum could turn this sort of situation into an excuse for an outing. She spoke to Wallis. 'Would you like some new shoes, dear?'

'Can we finish *Killer Zombies II* first?'

'Later maybe.' Mum sounded unusually hesitant. She'd obviously been losing. 'We'll go to Kendals for lunch.'

'The Green Rooms, Margaret,' Julia said, gathering jacket and car keys. 'On me, remember?'

Mum beamed.

'Don't you think you ought to tell AnnaMaria your plans?' I asked, helping Wallis with her coat.

Julia took a deep breath and retreated to the hall with her mobile. We listened in silence to her raised yet muffled voice.

Red-faced, she returned to the kitchen. 'No problem. She sends her blessing – ' a blatant lie, Julia was clearly rattled by the conversation – 'but wants the car for a service. Could you take us to town, Margaret?' she asked, turning to my elegant and sole-surviving parent.

38

Mum was flattered and gracious enough to hand Julia the keys to the BMW.

'I'll drive the Ford,' I offered. 'You two follow.'

'You're not going out like that, are you?' Mum asked quietly, halting proceedings.

'And why not?' I snapped back.

'Well, actually, Letty,' Julia chimed in, 'you've been a bit heavyhanded with the Eau-de-Chicken.'

It took me five minutes to shower and three minutes to dress. Mum looked delighted, Wallis couldn't have cared less and Julia did a double take when I reappeared.

It's not everyday I wear a skirt.

Left over from 1988, when the Banderas were my favourite band, my black skirt, white poloneck and long black jacket still looked cool enough for Manchester. DM shoes completed the look.

'Shall we go?' I suggested.

We left the warmth of the kitchen for the mud of the yard. It was a step up from snow, in my opinion.

Chapter 6

The trip to the garage was a treat. Wallis sang a medley of hits on the short drive over and her voice was as sweet as her face. My maternal instincts were at an all-time high.

The occasional glance in the mirror was proof enough that, at least for the moment, all was well in Julia's world. Animated and expressive, she handled my mother and the BMW with equal assurance. Given half a chance and an expense account, she'd have happily driven to her ancestral home in Italy.

AnnaMaria was fixing a car with a mallet when we arrived at the garage. I was relieved to see it wasn't my Land-Rover.

'Where is she?' she demanded as I pulled up beside the car she was demolishing. 'I'm going to fucking kill her.'

I struggled out of the car, my skirt limiting my range of movements. Opening the passenger door, I helped Wallis alight. Noticing the gleeful look in her eye, I hung onto her hand. If I didn't watch her, she'd be there with a mallet too.

'Whoa, AnnaMaria. What's up?'

I dangled the car keys in front of her and she snatched them from me, pausing momentarily to stare at my legs.

'Ms fucking Cosa Nostra. I'm going to bloody brain her.'

She clenched the mallet menacingly and Wallis shot behind my legs. I must admit I took a shuffle backwards myself. AnnaMaria's outbursts, though rare, were legendary. Lean, strong and wild-eyed, she wasn't someone to cross without good reason.

'Come on, AnnaMaria. What's happened?'

She took my arm with her wiry and grubby free hand and marched me into the office. Wallis trailed behind.

Decorated in the *Steptoe* style, the premises were a dream for any self-respecting car-boot fan or a nightmare, depending on your point of view. Julia hated it. Her new flat in the redeveloped Manchester suburb of Hulme, a mile or so from the city centre, was meticulously designed, furnished and organised. The garage was totally the opposite. Only AnnaMaria could find her way around the place. It wasn't so surprising that Julia managed to do most of her saleswork from home or by mobile. Only the forecourt, at the moment proudly boasting a two-year-old Nissan Micra, an Escort XR3i (in boy-racer black), several Cavaliers that, in truth, were the two women's bread and butter, and finally a thirty-year-old Bentley Eight, looked spruce.

Julia had 'a pain in her stomach' for the Bentley, as Anne, of distant Irish stock, was quick to quote. The fact that it did ten miles to the gallon (on a run) was the only thing that put her off. That and the eighteen-thousand-pounds asking price.

The Bentley – big, bold and sleekly dark grey – was an ex-funeral car which Julia had somehow 'acquired' from the Co-Op. The closeted lesbian funeral director was somehow involved, though I'd never asked how. Calderton Village was always alive with rumour and didn't need me to add to it.

AnnaMaria made space for me among the garage paraphernalia and directed me to a single (broken) office chair. On the desk was the local paper.

'Have you read this?' she demanded, tapping the pages angrily with a filthy finger. 'How much did she know about it?' she bellowed before I had a chance to answer. 'She's been avoiding telling me, knowing her. Always hiding her head in the sand. She thinks if she ignores something long enough it'll go away. She's so fucking . . .' The right word escaped her for a moment. 'Stupid,' was the best she could eventually manage, waving her arms around in a fury. She was still gripping the mallet.

'Don't you think you ought to speak to her first?' I asked, a bit shaken by her over-reaction. 'You shouldn't assume – '

'I can assume anything where she's concerned. And don't you worry, I'll be speaking to her all right, and if she thinks I'm doing any more work she's got another think coming.' She slammed down her weapon and ripped off her filthy overalls, revealing T-shirt and jeans. She rolled the greasy article into a ball and flung it at the filing cabinet. A potted plant went flying.

I quickly read the newspaper article again while Wallis attempted to save the damaged fern. The information in the newspaper was allegedly supplied by 'a source' at the Highway's Agency. Details of the proposed bypass were there in black and white. Still at the development stage, comments were welcome from the public.

'What did she say when she rang you?' I asked quietly.

'She reckoned the newspaper article was the first she'd heard. Huh! Fucking liar. The longer you leave things, the worse they get,' she stated obscurely.

'Yes, but nobody else has said anything. Surely someone would have heard.' This appeal for common sense fell on deaf ears.

'Is that her?' AnnaMaria demanded, as Mum's BMW drew smoothly into the drive.

She leapt to her feet, ready to do battle, and was out of the door and half-way down the path before I could stop her. Anyway, I didn't want to get involved in their fight. I only had one pair of tights. Wallis clung to me with one hand, the potted plant held tightly in the other. She reminded me of Drew Barrymore in *ET*.

'Why is she so mad?' she whispered.

I avoided the 'some people are like that' approach and told her, in language as uncomplicated as I could manage, about the newspaper article, the bypass and the rest of it. To my surprise, she laughed.

Raised voices outside had me risking a glance through the filthy office windows. Mum was bravely holding the two women apart and still she didn't have a hair out of place.

'Don't worry about the road, Letty,' Wallis insisted. 'We've done it loads of times before.'

'Yes, but did you ever win?' It was an idle question and one I didn't really expect an answer to. Wallis' reply taught me never to underestimate a five-year-old.

'Oh, yes. Laura says we always win.'

I glanced at Wallis, but before I had a chance to question the odd comment a bellow from outside caught my attention again.

Mum, temper finally lost, had whacked both women across the face. I held my breath at the sudden violence and waited for AnnaMaria to explode. Instead Mum wagged a stern finger at the pair of them and, shamefaced, they shook hands. It was too bizarre to be real.

'Let's pretend we didn't see them,' I suggested.

'Okay,' Wallis stage-whispered back.

We waltzed outside and tried to act normal. The trouble was, I couldn't look any of them in the eye and had to focus somewhere along hairlines.

'Shall we get going, then?' I said to Julia's forehead.

'I'll drive,' she muttered and clambered into the driver's side of the BMW. A red mark glowed faintly beneath her tanned skin.

Mum climbed in beside her as AnnaMaria locked up the garage. My Land-Rover was parked rather forlornly in one corner. I had the very real feeling I'd never drive her again.

'Don't you go without me,' AnnaMaria yelled as she checked the gates. Julia revved the engine out of spite and looked casually out of the side window. Mum, comfortably enthroned, finger-poked her in the ribs.

'Childish,' she muttered.

Finally satisfied with her security check, AnnaMaria sat in the back, sandwiching Wallis between us.

*

Manchester's sprawling masses seemed more sprawling than ever. Even at lunchtime thousands of people were milling about, as though the city was under some kind of siege.

The M62, leading through and beyond the middle-class suburbs of Prestwich, was backed up. Without having to see them, years of experience told me that Manchester's extremities would be packed with traffic. Stockport Road heading south, Oldham Street and Rochdale Road heading north, all bursting at the seams. Only the city centre, criss-crossed by tramways and bus lanes, was relatively free of cars. I was relieved. Four adults and a child trapped in a car, even one as richly endowed as Mum's BMW, would have been a nightmare had the traffic been really bad.

Julia, too tight to pay for a parking space, drove down High Street and past the Royal Exchange Theatre before throwing a left at Boots and turning into a tiny side road. To my disgust, she left the car in a disabled-parking slot. She even whisked a couple of orange badges from her jacket and left them on the dashboard.

'You should be ashamed of yourself,' I muttered as I edged out of the car, being careful not to snag my tights. I remembered then why I always wore trousers.

'I've got a heart condition,' Julia replied stuffily.

'You will have when I've finished with you,' Anna-Maria threatened quietly.

'Now, girls,' Mum protested, helping Wallis to disembark. 'Let's not have any arguing. And, Julia, I really don't think you should park here.'

Mum was on high moral ground but Julia valiantly tried to save face. 'Only last year I was rushed to hospital with chest pains!'

'Julia!' I howled. 'You had wind.'

Her face flushed and, caught by the truth, she climbed back into the car. 'All right,' she snapped. 'I'm going home to get changed. I'll see you in the Green Rooms in about an hour. At least you can park there,' she added quietly but with some malice. Then she slammed the door and shot off in a cloud of exhaust.

AnnaMaria cackled. One small victory for her.

'Right, ladies. Shoes, I think,' Mum ordered and, taking command of Wallis, marched off in the direction of Market Street.

Chapter 7

'So what's happening with Wallis?' AnnaMaria asked as we trailed after Mum.

The roads were madness. Hundreds of office workers in search of the perfect sandwich were at large, interspersed with kids off school (skiving rather than half-term). Manchester's population seemed to have tripled in minutes.

Swiftly side-stepping a speeding pram, I delved into my jacket pocket and produced the note from Laura.

'So they're tree people?' AnnaMaria said, scanning the brief paragraph.

'I suppose.' I sighed, scurrying after the shopper and her charge. 'Precious few trees on Batley Close though,' I observed.

We took a left into Market Street. A sea of sun-denied faces headed in our direction. This was worse than the January sales. AnnaMaria slipped her leather-jacketed arm through mine and raised her voice above the din.

'So it's something they do often?'

'Well, there was some mention of it when I spoke to her yesterday.' God, was it only yesterday? 'I didn't realise it was a crusade though. And she didn't say anything about the local bypass.'

'You didn't know anything about any of it, did you?' There was an unfamiliar urgency in AnnaMaria's voice.

I glanced at her striking Annie Lennox features and realised she was more worried than mad now.

'No, not really. There was some talk of it ages ago – you knew about that – but the last I'd heard, the plans had been scrapped. It's odd that they have been dusted off again.'

'Yeah, well, you know what they're like.'

'They' covered every aspect of officialdom: the DSS, the tax office, Health and Safety. AnnaMaria even had a suspicious dislike of dinner ladies (she'd got food poisoning at her local comprehensive and had lived off her own cheese and onion sandwiches for her last three years of school life).

Suddenly she stopped dead in her tracks and stared at HMV's windows. Then she hauled me through the crowds for a closer look.

'My God, she's on at the Apollo!' she exclaimed breathlessly.

'Who?' I asked, scanning the lists of forthcoming attractions. Elkie Brooks was doing another farewell tour and Shirley Bassey was sold out at Nynex Arena, but much as I liked the two chanteuses, I very much doubted they'd take AnnaMaria's breath away.

'Kim Stove.' She said the name reverentially. A name I'd never heard.

'Who?' I asked once again.

'Kim Stove,' she repeated loudly, lengthening the surname.

'I've heard of Betty Stove, the tennis player,' I said stupidly, though I couldn't imagine why she'd be on at the Apollo.

'No. Kim, the poet.'

Kim the poet?

'I didn't know you liked poetry.'

'I don't,' AnnaMaria said.

'So . . .'

'She's more than just a poet, she's . . .'

AnnaMaria obviously didn't have words to express her feelings.

'Come on,' she ordered, dragging me into the shop and up the moving staircase.

We were surrounded by twelve-year-old pickpockets and I clung to my shoulder bag as we surged along to join a long queue of silent fans waiting for tickets.

'Have you got your credit card?' AnnaMaria asked impatiently.

'Yes. Why?' Stupid question really.

'Buy two tickets for me and I'll owe you.'

I sighed. 'All right.' I rummaged in my bag, beyond arguing. 'How much are they?'

'Thirty-five quid.'

'Each?' I choked loudly.

A couple of hippie types glared at me. We weren't so much in a record shop as in a church.

'Yes, but she hardly ever does concerts. And for her to be in England . . .' She paused, overcome by events. 'Anyway, I'll pay you back, don't worry.' She looked agitatedly at the distant ticket booths.

'Who's the other one for?'

'You,' she stated simply.

I'd never heard of Kim Stove. Whoever she was and however good she was, the tickets were outrageously priced. What's more, I was paying for them, but somehow I was very touched.

'You'll love her,' AnnaMaria stated and suddenly frogmarched me to an empty booth.

'Two for Kim Stove.' That breathless tone again.

The woman behind the counter shook her head as she scanned the computer screen for available seats. My companion hopped from one foot to the other as the assistant paused, answered an insistent phone and then turned back to us after a moment.

'Ah,' she said.

'Ah,' AnnaMaria replied.

'Two seats left, not a bad view. You're lucky. Somebody just died and cancelled.'

Gruesome and strange. Did they cancel and then die, or the other way round? If the latter, who cancelled? AnnaMaria pulled my Visa card from between my sweaty fingers.

'Chop, chop, Letty.' She was grinning from ear to ear. 'Sign the thing.'

Seconds later we were back on the street, two tickets safely in the depths of AnnaMaria's Levi's.

We found Mum and Wallis easily enough. The assistants running around like headless chickens gave the game away.

'I want them measuring.' Mum's voice would have chilled Vincent Price. 'Just because she looks like a size 8 doesn't mean she is, does it dear?'

Shelley's shoeshop had never seen the like and a measuring device was produced from the depths of the storeroom.

Little Wallis was as thrilled with the attention as AnnaMaria had been with the tickets.

'Can I have red ones, Mrs Margaret, please?'

'You can have any colour you like, dear, as long as they fit. Now, what about those Kicker boots you've taken a fancy to? Let's see if they've got your size.'

As a pale-faced gofer shot past me to fetch the required style, Mum spotted us. 'Where did you two get to?' she demanded, rapidly lacing a pair of cute Pod shoes.

'I managed to get tickets for Kim,' AnnaMaria stated proudly.

Mum's response was astonishing. 'My goodness,' she said. 'You lucky thing. I tried last week, but they said it was sold out.'

'Somebody died,' AnnaMaria said happily. 'I'm taking Letty.'

Mum smiled warmly – not the most common of events. 'Letitia, you'll love her. AnnaMaria, I'll give you some money. You must get me a T-shirt.'

Was this a conspiracy? What was I missing, for God's sake?

Mum spotted my face and her smile became broader. 'I've got some tapes you can borrow. Listen to them before the concert next week. You don't know what a delight you've got in store.'

That was true enough. I hadn't the faintest idea.

*

Two pairs of shoes were bought in the end. Somehow Mum even got a discount and the best service this side of Harrods, while AnnaMaria and I were left to gaze longingly at boots we could never afford.

'Can I keep these on, Mrs Margaret?' Wallis enquired as Mum signed a cheque.

'Oh, you must,' she said and took charge of the second parcel, having handed over Wallis' ancient wellies to the assistant with a grimace and a 'Burn these, would you?'

He took them from her gingerly, between two fingers, and we were seen off the premises like royalty. I had a feeling they were glad to see the back of us.

Mum and Wallis had further shopping expeditions in mind and we agreed that, should we become separated, we'd meet up in the Green Rooms.

We made our way through the thinning crowds and I took the opportunity to ask AnnaMaria something I'd been meaning to ask all day.

'What did you make of Laura?'

Office workers scurried past us, clutching their shopping and heading back to temperamental VDUs and equally temperamental bosses.

'I dunno,' she said thoughtfully. 'It's a bit odd meeting a long-last aunt and it is a tragic story. It's funny, but even though everyone found her a bit difficult, I always got on all right with Granny Marple. I must have been the only one! But it's how you act, isn't it, not who you are?' She looked at me for confirmation.

I shrugged. Too deep for me.

'I mean, I know Wallis isn't Laura's kid, but she's been involved in her upbringing long enough.' She paused and shook her head sadly. 'To abandon her like that.'

'You like her, don't you?'

'Wallis? God, she's gorgeous.'

'Ever fancy having kids yourself?'

'What, with Andy?' she asked with a laugh.

AnnaMaria was the first to admit he was a bit gormless, though sweet enough. They'd been seeing each other since she was seventeen, so something obviously held them together.

'Well, whoever,' I urged, eager to hear her views on motherhood.

'I'd adopt Wallis, no problem,' she said evasively and turned away with a smile.

Marks was in sight but a policewoman was holding back the hordes at the bottom of Market Street as a cavalcade of limousines drove slowly past. We edged our way to the front in an effort to keep Mum in sight, but of course she'd disappeared. Having precedence over the lights, the drivers of the cars were in no rush. I peered into the back of one, the little flags adorning its bonnet announcing a Very Important Person indeed. I raised a hand in mischievous salute and Julia waved back at me through the reinforced glass.

'Did you see that? It wasn't just me, was it?'

'No,' AnnaMaria said, sighing. 'I saw her too.'

The policewoman finally waved us on as I stared after the vehicles in amazement. AnnaMaria, fazed by no one, collared the policewoman on the way across.

'Who were they?' she asked.

'Sita Joshi,' came the short reply. 'And the mayoress.'

We were dismissed as the policewoman went about her business. The crowds carried us across the road and into Marks' front door before I could address AnnaMaria.

'Who the hell's Sita Joshi?'

'That new MP,' she said, clearly exasperated. 'Letty, don't you read anything?'

'Not if I can help it,' I muttered.

'And before you ask, I don't know what Julia was doing in that car. All right?'

Stung, I said, 'Well, there's no need to bite my head off.'

AnnaMaria lowered her gorgeous hazel eyes and promptly burst into tears. She pulled her leather jacket tighter around her slim body. She was a picture of dejection and all I could do was put my arms around her.

'AnnaMaria, whatever's wrong?'

Her shoulders heaved in reply. The security guards were giving us curious sidelong glances.

'Come on, let's have a cup of tea.' My hand chanced against her bare neck. 'You're freezing,' I added. 'Are you ill? Is it your period? You are a bit pale.'

Her shoulders heaved some more and it took me a moment to realise her tears had turned to laughter. Slightly hysterical laughter, but laughter all the same. Eyes wet with tears, her mouth displayed a wobbly smile.

'Tea, yeah, I'd love one.' She swallowed a last sob and, taking her hand, I led her from the store.

We didn't go to the Green Rooms straight away. AnnaMaria couldn't face my mother (I knew exactly how she felt), so we took temporary refuge at one of the downstairs cafés in the Royal Exchange.

This strange complex where Victoriana meets nineties rave was a rustling, bustling warren of gift shops and Belgian-chocolate sellers. Tiny stalls stocking a wonderful array of toys from years gone by traded next to shops with a more twentieth-century feel; bath oils made from every fruit known to man added to the already pungent odour of second-hand clothes and 'pre-enjoyed' furniture. And, of course, the high-class tobacconist was still doing good business. Home to a blonde sales assistant, her voluptuous figure and Louise Brooks face had been a continuing fantasy throughout my office-worker years. A traitorous thought and one I would never act on, but maybe I could buy Julia some cigs on the way out. On second thoughts, she could buy her own, judging by the company she was keeping. My God, I couldn't wait to hear her story.

I bought tea for two, proper designer cups and saucers and a dinky teapot, not quite the mugs and tea-bags we had at home.

AnnaMaria had recovered her composure, though she was still a bit blotchy and green around the gills. I didn't have to ask her again what was wrong.

'I'm pregnant,' she said shortly as she stirred her tea.

'Good Lord,' I said. A prissy comment but comfortably noncommittal.

'About ten weeks,' she added, unprompted. 'And it's not Andy's.'

'Oh,' I replied, wishing we'd gone to the pub instead. 'Congratulations?' I ventured.

'Thanks,' she said and laughed. 'You're the first to know, Letty. I should have told Anne, but I only found out for definite today. I got a call from Dr Weiss.'

'And how do you feel?'

'Happy, nauseous, worried, excited.'

'Fairly normal, then,' I said with a smile. 'Can I ask – '

'No one you know,' AnnaMaria interrupted hurriedly. 'No one anyone knows. It was just a fling. Andy knows about it, though he doesn't know about the baby.' She stopped suddenly and I could almost feel her trying out the word for size. She smiled to herself and an unsteady hand slid to her stomach.

'Will you tell him?'

'Yes,' she said decisively. 'He can have a say in the relationship, but not on my body.'

Powerful stuff, this reproduction lark.

'I take it you're keeping it, then?'

She nodded and I could see tears were close again.

'It goes without saying you can stay put, you know. The farm will always be your home. You could use the loft if you like. There's plenty of room.'

I knew without asking that Anne would support me in this. AnnaMaria looked at me gratefully and tears spilled from her bottom lids. I could have cried with her, but instead passed her a bundle of paper napkins.

There was silence for a moment and, despite the bombshell, the world carried on as usual.

'So what now?'

'Well,' she began, crunching up the napkins, 'I don't want anyone else to know until I've told Andy. I don't know what will happen with him, but there are more important considerations now.'

She paused again and rattled a spoon in her cup while she gathered her thoughts.

'I want to carry on working, presuming we've still got

a garage when the baby's born. And if we have, I'll hire somebody while I'm off. I'll think of something. Do you know anything about mechanics, Letty?' she asked mischievously.

'No. Chickens are my forte,' I said, laughing. 'I know it's early days yet, but, assuming the worst happens, what will you do if the garage has to go?' I asked her.

AnnaMaria leaned back in her seat and shrugged. 'I suppose there'll be compensation and we could start again, though we're well established where we are. It's Julia I'm worried about.'

Excuse me while I faint.

'I shouldn't worry too much. She never sinks for long.'

'Yeah, but she's not getting any younger, is she?'

I spluttered into my tea. 'I wouldn't say that to her face if I were you. She's forty-two, not ninety-two.'

'You know what I mean,' she said, smiling.

'Things will change a bit,' I went on. As an understatement, it was this year's prize contender.

'Yeah.' AnnaMaria looked anywhere but at me. 'How are you with nappies?'

I snorted derisively, though the idea of baby-sitting, especially for AnnaMaria, wasn't so horrendous.

We would have to wait and see.

Chapter 8

It was packed in the Green Rooms. The first half of the afternoon matinée had just finished and the theatre's patrons were hogging the bar. Julia was holding court of a different kind. The limousines that had passed us on Market Street were lined up outside the building and the chauffeurs, taking the opportunity for a quick fag, were leaning against the cars.

All but one.

A woman driver, noticeable by her aloofness, stood by her charge, almost at attention. Her black peaked cap (a fitting addition to her sleek black uniform) was pulled low over eyes that missed nothing. Tall and muscular, she was at odds with her surroundings. A small earpiece, such as those worn by TV presenters, nestled comfortably over one small pink lobe. A tiny trail of wire leading from it disappeared under her jacket collar. She was a figure from a Jack Higgins novel and she gave me the creeps.

'Stop gawping, Letty,' AnnaMaria scolded. 'Haven't

you ever seen a bodyguard before?'

'Well, actually, no,' I confessed.

'Come on,' she insisted and stepped through the automatic glass doors that led to the bar.

We were hit by a barrage of sound.

'I don't think I can stand much of this,' AnnaMaria murmured into my ear. We were at the room's centre and were being jostled just for standing space. 'Are you bothered about staying?' she asked.

'Me? No.' I'd had enough of Manchester for one day.

AnnaMaria pulled a face. 'Come on, then. As tempting as it is to let Julia pay for lunch, on the whole I'd much rather be in Calderton. I'm knackered.'

I immediately wanted to take her home and pamper her.

AnnaMaria pointed upstairs. 'We'd better tell your mother if we're going, though. Look, they're up there.'

The upstairs gallery was cordoned off for a private party. The mayoress, in all her finery, was instantly recognisable, as was my mother, who was bending her ear.

Julia was flirting with an Asian woman and Wallis was drowning under a sea of ice cream. Other dignitaries milled about, eating and drinking freebies.

'We're not going to get up there, are we?' I said, warily eyeing the heavily built bodyguard standing at the foot of the stairs.

'Ring Julia,' AnnaMaria suggested. 'On her mobile. Go on. There's a public phone near the bar.'

'Oh, for God's sake!' I laughed. 'I keep expecting Emma Peel to walk through the door.'

I did as I was told, though.

'Hello?' Julia said.

59

The laughter in the background came through in stereo. I was hearing it live and via BT simultaneously.

'Julia, it's Letty.'

'Hiya,' she said happily. 'Saw you going into Marks. Did you get anything nice?'

'Only a headache,' I moaned over the noise.

'What?' Julia bellowed.

'Nothing,' I replied, not wanting to repeat myself. 'We're downstairs. We're off home. AnnaMaria's tired.'

'My God, she must be ill,' was Julia's observation.

'What shall we do about Wallis?' I said, changing the subject speedily.

'Oh we'll drop her off later. You'll never believe who I'm with,' Julia said, chuckling.

The phone crackled with static.

'Tell me tonight, Julia. This line's terrible. Just make sure Wallis is home in time for tea.'

'Don't worry. She'll be fine. She's having a great time.'

The line faded a bit more, then went dead. I glanced up to find Julia leaning over the balcony.

'I'll come down,' she mouthed.

I pointed to the door, away from the theatregoers.

Despite the main road, the pavement outside the Green Rooms was comparatively quiet and the cold air was a relief after the smoky atmosphere. I suddenly felt crushingly old.

Julia and Wallis came bursting through the doors. Wallis immediately wrapped herself around AnnaMaria's legs. I must admit I felt a twinge of envy.

'Letty, I've met the mayor,' she squealed delightedly. 'Is that like the Queen?' Her eyes were wide with excitement.

AnnaMaria opened her mouth to slag off all things royal.

'Sort of,' I said hurriedly, stopping the tirade.

Julia, for all her sophistication, was no better. 'You'll never guess who my neighbour is,' she chortled.

'Surprise me,' I said.

'The Honourable Member for Caldervale West, Sita Joshi,' she crowed.

'She lives in Hulme?' AnnaMaria asked, aghast, hoisting Wallis onto her shoulders. 'Is she mad? Why doesn't she live nearer her electorate?' Itching for a fight, AnnaMaria knew just how to needle Julia.

'It's not the dump it used to be. And why shouldn't she live in Manchester?' Julia asked sniffily. 'She can tend to her voters needs just as easily from there.'

Julia had bought a flat in Hulme after her affair with the Scandinavian woman had taken a nosedive.(Actually her Abba-esque partner had almost ended up in prison on smuggling charges, but that's another story altogether.)

Nobody in their right mind would have bought a property in this notorious suburb a couple of years prior to redevelopment and even Julia had realised problems don't disappear overnight. Smackheads don't stop taking drugs just because they've got a new house, and a mugger isn't going to give up his night job for the sake of a new sink unit. But for all that the city's investment in a dying area had paid dividends. Private housing rubbed shoulders with council and housing association properties and small businesses shared resources with enterprising co-ops. Suddenly there was more to inner-city life than drugs and gangsters.

*

'How come you ended up in the Daimler?' I asked Julia curiously, eyeing the fancy car and its aloof chauffeur.

'It's like I said, she's a neighbour. We were heading in the same direction.'

Julia sighed. She expected all to be clear without explanation. I think she had me down as Mystic Meg.

'She was supposed to be chairing that meeting tomorrow, about the bypass, but it's been postponed. There's been a big fuss about the news being leaked to the papers. Especially since nothing is certain yet.' She looked at AnnaMaria meaningfully. 'She's pushing for a venue in Calderton so all the local people involved can have their say, but it'll be a while before it can be arranged. You know how long these things take.'

'And since when have you been such an expert?' I asked incredulously.

AnnaMaria opened her mouth to add her own comments, but weariness got the better of her. She'd been in this frustrating position with Julia before.

'So come on, then, what's the news?' I asked on AnnaMaria's behalf.

'There isn't any really,' Julia admitted. 'We'll have to see what happens at the meeting.'

'You know who we could ask?' AnnaMaria interrupted.

'Who?' Julia asked, suspiciously. The ball was in her court and she wasn't about to hand it back.

'Our friendly neighbourhood shopkeeper, Mrs Buckham. Doesn't her niece work for the *Echo*?'

'A junior position,' Julia pointed out.

'I'll ask,' I offered, before the knives came out. 'I'll ring her about it later.'

Of course, I never did.

A sudden breeze whipped around our legs and cold spots of rain began to fall on our unprotected heads.

'Come on, AnnaMaria. Let's get you home,' I said without thinking, but Julia, too wrapped up in herself, missed it.

'The car's at my place. You can leave it at the garage. Don't worry, I'll sort your mum and Wallis out,' she said, easing Wallis from AnnaMaria's shoulders.

Julia was extraordinarily gentle with the little girl. Wallis really did bring out the best in all of us.

'Here are the car keys,' Julia said, producing them from her jacket pocket. 'Sapphire will give you a lift to the flat.'

Sapphire? We were going home on a horse?

The chauffeur, she of the horsy name but far from horsy features, acknowledged us with a small salute and the dark eyes gazed speculatively at AnnaMaria, who returned the look with a slight smile. Odd.

'Are you sure, Julia?' I said, eyeing the driver.

Julia waved away my objections. 'Sita won't mind,' she said with a grin.

I knew that grin. It was a fair bet that the new MP for CalderVale was about to become a bit more than just Julia's neighbour.

'In fact, you can help yourself to dinner if you like. I know you missed out today.' Julia began edging her way back into the bar, Wallis clinging like a koala. 'There's a pizza to die for in the fridge and, AnnaMaria,' she said finally before slipping from sight, 'There's a present for you. You can't miss it.'

The door closed behind her.

'My God,' AnnaMaria spluttered. 'She never buys me anything, not even for the garage. She's worse than Gladys Althorpe.'

I was stumped by her lateral thinking for a moment, until images of the Boddington's advert came to mind.

'Come on, Letty,' she urged. 'Let's see what it is,' and she dragged me over to a waiting Sapphire.

I'd never sat in a limo before, much less a chauffeur-driven one. The nearest I'd been was Manchester's own lesbian taxi service, Elles Belles, a potential gossip column on wheels if only the cabbies weren't so tight-lipped.

A slightly darkened screen and the back of Sapphire's neck prevented a clear view through the windscreen. Not that I particularly wanted to see where I was going, the interior of the car was far too interesting for that. The navy leather seats could accommodate at least six and, enjoying a luxurious extra, AnnaMaria was engrossed in Sky TV on the set built into the back of the passenger seat.

I tapped on the screen for Sapphire's attention. The quietest of hums and the glass partition slid open to reveal a clearer picture of her head. We made eye contact in the rear-view mirror.

'Yes, ma'am?' she murmured in a low tone.

I cleared my voice. 'Whose car is this exactly?' I asked of those mysterious and, I must admit, rather sexy eyes.

'It's Ms Joshi's private car, ma'am. She uses it mostly in her official capacity.'

'Yes, but what – '

The car phone flickered into life.

'Excuse me, ma'am,' Sapphire said and, as she reached for the hand set, the screen slid back into place with a whoosh.

AnnaMaria glanced sideways at me, an odd smirk on her lips. 'Ma'am, is it now?'

'I know,' I said. 'I'm finally getting the respect I deserve.'

The smirk turned into a laugh and the laugh to giggles on the short journey to Hulme.

Julia's flat was situated half-way up Chorlton Road. Reasonably priced to encourage professionals like Julia to move into the area, it lay just a couple of hundred yards north of Trafford (cheap Council Tax) and a mile or so east of Chorlton Village (inflated house prices and opinion of its trendy self).

Julia's mother had forked out for the property – not for the first time either in Julia's somewhat chequered financial career. It's as well they're related, otherwise I'm sure that, sooner or later, Shergar's head would have ended up on Julia's pillow.

Sadly the journey was over almost before it began. We'd caught all the green lights and, not so surprisingly, other drivers had been almost deferential in their treatment of us.

Sapphire was a wonderfully calm driver and as we drew up outside Julia's place I was tempted to ask her to take us for a run round the block.

Instead, AnnaMaria invited her up for a coffee. I looked at her in surprise. Turned sideways on, with her chin resting on the back of the passenger seat, AnnaMaria looked imploringly at Sapphire's handsome features.

The driver hesitated.

'You can spare five minutes,' AnnaMaria urged.

Sapphire turned in her seat to face her and smiled. My surprise of moments before turned to astonishment.

'Come on, darlin', for old times' sake.'

Sapphire laughed, a full throaty sound, and reached up to remove her cap. Thick, dark hair fell to her shoulders.

Framed by her luxurious mane of hair, Sapphire's Slavic origins became apparent. Heavy brows accentuated the gentle upward slope of her eyes; coupled with high cheekbones, this was the stuff of supermodels. There was nothing exotic about the accent, though. Her Yorkshire dialect was one of the broadest I'd ever heard.

'I should coco,' she said obscurely in her flat but not unpleasant voice.

She smiled at me and I was forced to revise my first impressions of her as a Jack Higgins moll.

AnnaMaria spluttered with laughter at her strange comment.

'You don't remember her, do you, Letty?'

Bewildered, I shook my head.

'Substitute Tracey for Sapphire,' she suggested.

I shrugged, no wiser.

'Calder Valley High?' AnnaMaria pressed.

A pinpoint of light began to appear somewhere in the back of my mind.

'A nature weekend? Working farms of Britain?'

The pinpoint became a floodlight.

'My God,' I gasped and laughed with the memory. 'Bald, skinny, piercings?'

Sapphire, a.k.a. Tracey, stuck her tongue out. 'Dat's all

'I'th got letht,' she stammered, pointing to a steel ball an inch from the end of her tongue. 'Well, all you can see at any rate,' she added with a smile. 'I can't wear the rest for this job.'

'What happened to you, Trace? Or is it Sapphire now?' AnnaMaria asked her old schoolfriend. 'This is the first time I've seen you since you were expelled.'

Tracey raised her hand in denial. 'No, no,' she said. 'I left before they had the chance. And yes, it's Sapphire. Tracey's well in the past now.'

'Was she pushed or did she fall?' AnnaMaria chortled.

'Did George ever recover from that weekend?' Sapphire asked with a grin.

George has the neighbouring farm. He's as old as God and has the same unpredictable temperament. He was the last person I would have expected to volunteer his educational services, but there was some money in it, so perhaps it wasn't that strange after all. At the time he'd had a couple of pre-BSE milkers, a goat, which he used in the same way a normal person would use a lawn mower, half a dozen fat and ageing chickens and a partridge in a pear tree. Oh, and a dog so fat and mangy no one would touch it. Even the goat was overweight. I thought it was a physical impossibility to overfeed a goat, but this one – Billy, would you believe? – was enormous.

When George finally did get some money for his community spirit, he found it wasn't nearly enough to compensate him for all the trouble he'd had. Teenage animal rights activists do not as a rule take kindly to farming practices of the twentieth century, even if those practices are as ineffectual as George's.

I didn't know AnnaMaria at the time. I knew of her, of

course, though her reputation as a Lolita was, I found out later, completely unfounded. Her reputation for trouble, however, wasn't. Her notoriety was something the Stones in the sixties could only have dreamed about.

She was born too late to be a punk and too early for its revival. She'd flirted with the rave scene for a while, though the accompanying drugs did her head in. Her mum had died at the hands of a drugged-up driver and she had unshakeable views on that. So trapped somewhere in the non-political early nineties, AnnaMaria and Tracey too had developed a style all of their own.

Their campaign of terror was heavily influenced by the Baader-Meinhof Gang and Carlos the Jackal. The only thing they didn't do was hold old George to ransom, but only because they knew no one would a) miss him and b) pay up.

Within an hour of arrival they'd broken into the cow shed and liberated Jane and Janet, the elderly Jersey cows. The chickens were also released from their shabby coop into the wilderness that was George's farm. I found the cows in my back garden, eating my ripening crop of strawberries. A couple of the hens came to a sadder end. Somehow mistaken for pheasants, local poachers had put enough shot in them to break every filling in a person's head. I felt sorry for George and ended up replacing his chickens with a couple of reliable layers of my own. AnnaMaria's visit had taken ten years off his life.

Tracey's efforts had had a much more sinister hue. She wanted to blow up the cowshed. Despite her *Anarchists' Handbook*, her plans had thankfully gone awry. The incendiary device, made from fertiliser, was too unstable and the only things she managed to destroy were her own non-animal-product boots. And that's why George found her floundering in the rain barrel by the side of the cowshed, the dog alternately barking and throwing up in excitement.

The racket had brought me running – sound travels quite clearly across the farmyard – and a phone call to AnnaMaria's Auntie Anne had her swiftly on the scene. It was the first time, incidentally, that Anne and I exchanged more than just a few words, though our affair began much later.

Tracey's parents, Romanies staying temporarily in the area, were informed, though we kept the gossip from the rest of the village – some were prejudiced enough already and a barn-burning exercise would only incite them to riot.

AnnaMaria kept her head down for a while and I'd never seen Tracey – sorry, Sapphire – again until now.

'So where did you go?' AnnaMaria asked.

'God, everywhere,' Sapphire began.

'Well, come upstairs then and tell us all about it,' AnnaMaria pressed, reaching for Sapphire's hand and giving it a gentle but insistent tug.

Once more that slight hesitation and then Sapphire smiled thoughtfully at her former friend. 'Oh, go on, then, just for five minutes. I wouldn't mind seeing this Julia's flat. She's an odd one, though. Ms Joshi seems quite taken with her. I don't know why, at such short notice,' she added, a trace of sharpness in her voice. 'I'll just call Harry – my colleague,' she explained.

Sapphire pressed a finger to her earpiece and

mumbled something into her sleeve. I've seen *Mission: Impossible*, I know a transmitter when I see one. Even so, I was quite impressed, and from AnnaMaria's expression she was too.

After a moment Sapphire replaced her cap. 'They'll be at the Green Rooms a while,' she explained. 'But I'm wanted for another function tonight. So I'll have to stick to five minutes. Maybe we can get together some time over a pint. As long as I'm not still barred from the local.'

AnnaMaria laughed. 'Well, you know what memories are like in Calderton.'

Sapphire, experience showing, slid smoothly from the car and opened the back door of the limo with a flourish.

'Madam,' she said, touching her cap.

Even a few Hulme curtains twitched at that. Despite their 'seen it all, done it all' world-weary air, the inhabitants of Julia's close could still be curious should a VIP appear on their doorstep. The disappointment was palpable when AnnaMaria and I stepped out.

We made a quick dash from the car to the main entrance. It wasn't getting any warmer as the day wore on and my stockinged legs were freezing.

Sapphire produced a swipe card that allowed us access to the entrance hall. She exchanged a few words with the uniformed doorman as she signed us in.

'Ms Joshi got me one. You know, for work,' she said, explaining the card. 'I run her about at all sorts of times.'

'Do you always have the limo, then?' AnnaMaria was back on her favourite subject.

'Nah, 'fraid not. I have to rely on my Mini,' Sapphire replied wistfully. 'She likes to drive the Daimler herself sometimes.'

'I'm not surprised,' AnnaMaria murmured, and for a moment they silently contemplated this dream of a car as the lift delivered us to Julia's door.

I'd been to Julia's place before, shortly after she'd moved in, when her mother had been over from Italy to help sort out the finances. It was odd, but whenever I was with her mother I never dropped my aitches and I'd rather cut my tongue out than swear. Sophia, the *grande dame* of polite Italian society, had made quite an impact. Julia got her sense of style from her mother, and her good looks. She'd taken me to her bosom in much the same way my mum had done with Julia. I've got more silk in my wardrobe than Willie Carson – a thousand scarves I will never wear.

Her dad was from a different mould altogether. I'd met him twice, once while holidaying in Italy, when he'd insisted on speaking English, and the last time in England, when he'd spoken nothing but Italian. A strange, intense man with a mobile phone constantly stuck to his ear, he'd have got on well with my mother.

I opened the walnut-veneer door with Julia's spare key. You've heard of quasi-semi? Well, this was quasi-loft. It was built into roof space all right – the wooden rafters were there for all to see – but that's where the similarity ended. A spiral staircase wound its way from the open lounge/diner to a bedroom perched precariously in mid-air. Only the kitchen (kitchenette, my gran would have called it) had any sort of division from the rest of the flat, a three-quarter plasterboard partition offering at least some privacy. Call me old-fashioned, but I like walls and a ceiling. And if I fall out of bed drunk, I don't want a twenty-foot drop onto my kitchen units.

AnnaMaria thought it was fantastic, not that she was likely to tell Julia. Ten cool points straight down the drain if she did.

'It's the same as Ms Joshi's,' Sapphire observed. 'Except the decor,' she added wryly, taking in Julia's rather erotic prints.

'Do you think Julia and your boss will get together, then?' AnnaMaria asked to my surprise. She wasn't usually that interested in lesbian gossip and even less when it concerned Julia.

Sapphire shrugged and somewhere behind those eyes a barrier slammed shut. AnnaMaria didn't press her.

'Where's my present, then?' AnnaMaria broke the awkward silence and looked around the flat expectantly.

'I've a feeling that's it,' I said, pointing to an unmistakable object behind the front door.

'Oh,' AnnaMaria managed quietly.

'Something you're not telling us?' Sapphire quipped, fingering the ribbon wrapped around the hood of the baby buggy.

'How the hell did she find out?' AnnaMaria bellowed, glaring in my direction.

'Don't look at me. When have I had chance to tell her? I only found out myself this afternoon, remember?'

Sapphire looked on, a strange expression on her face. I could have been wrong, but the slight shake of her head had a tinge of sadness about it.

'There's a note,' she said quietly, and handed it to the pregnant one.

'"Throwing up every morning for a fortnight was a dead giveaway. I don't know how Letty missed it. There's champagne in the fridge. Congratulations.'" AnnaMaria read.

I ignored Julia's comment and made for the fridge, though the alcohol was wasted a bit. I alone toasted the buggy and AnnaMaria's impending event, neither woman was inclined to join me. What a waste of a bottle of Bollinger. Sapphire had no intentions of wrapping herself or her boss around a lamppost and AnnaMaria would be alcohol-free for the foreseeable future.

Sapphire stayed five minutes, as promised, though AnnaMaria gleaned as much information from her as she could.

'I've been working for Ms Joshi for a while now, mostly as a bodyguard.'

'She's not been an MP for long, though, has she?' I queried.

Sapphire smiled. 'I know,' she said. 'But you must have heard of her.'

I hadn't, but my companion had.

'Of course, she is *that* Joshi, isn't she?' AnnaMaria declared.

I looked from one woman to the other.

'She used to be a film director,' she explained to me.

I pretended to look knowledgeable, though 'finger on the pulse' wasn't usually a phrase linked to my name.

'I thought she went out with Kim?' AnnaMaria pressed a reluctant Sapphire. The shutters slammed down again.

'Kim?' I asked brightly.

'Stove, who we're going to see next week.'

I smiled and went into the kitchen for more champagne. Perhaps AnnaMaria would translate the conversation into a language I could understand later.

I rummaged in Julia's fridge while AnnaMaria quizzed her friend further. The monster-sized pizza flung itself at me. Uncharacteristically, Julia had opted for a vegetarian selection. Twelve minutes and we'd be eating.

Sapphire declined the offer of food and instead made moves to leave. I retrieved her jacket while she had an intense conversation with AnnaMaria, a conversation I wasn't privy to, being kitchen-bound.

'It's been great seeing you again, Trace,' AnnaMaria said, using her old name still. 'And we'll get together for a drink soon.'

I held Sapphire's jacket while she threaded her muscular arms into the sleeves. Unnoticed by her, my hand brushed against something hard under her left arm, something unmistakable.

A gun.

Chapter 9

I managed not to say anything until she'd gone, though my stomach had dropped thirty floors at the unexpected discovery.

AnnaMaria saw her old friend to the car and, unable to resist, I went up the spiral staircase to have a good look through Julia's bedroom window. Any fool could see that their conversation was intense. At one point fingers were wagged and, though I couldn't hear, words were snapped in obvious anger. Propped against the car, arms crossed for warmth, AnnaMaria's head hung down as Sapphire leaned over her. I struggled and failed to open the locked porthole window before I realised just how nosy I was being. I caught a glimpse of Sapphire clutching at AnnaMaria's hands before I retreated downstairs.

When AnnaMaria returned ten minutes later, I pinned her to the wall with questions, managing to avoid the personal ones.

'How do I know if it's legal?' she said, dodging past me

and making for the steaming pizza. 'Perhaps everybody has a gun in Hulme nowadays.'

I joined her at the wrought-iron dining table. Julia's tastes had changed dramatically since her move to the city. Gone were the soft furnishings and William Morris patterns, replaced by hard wooden floors and metal furniture.

Fine if you wanted trouble with your kidneys. Give me a LemSip sofa any day.

AnnaMaria refused to speak during the meal. She put a Marianne Faithfull album on the turntable and that despairing voice managed to drown me out. It wasn't until we were in the car heading home, buggy packed in the boot, that we managed a conversation again.

'It probably is legal,' she conceded as we wound our way through heavy motorway traffic. 'She's a bodyguard, after all, and to a very controversial figure.'

'Oh?' I asked, intrigued. 'How so?'

She sighed, too tired and too pregnant to get into my way of thinking. The *Die Hard* school of thought, she called it.

'I don't suppose you read last Saturday's *Guardian*?' she asked, knowing my abhorrence of the news.

I answered anyway. 'No.'

'Well, there's an article on her in that. I've got it at work. I'll let you have it.'

'Give us a clue.'

'No. Read it for yourself.'

She switched the radio on. BBC Radio Five Live were reviewing the weekend's football matches and there was no talking through that.

★

Whoever said 'Home is where the heart is' wasn't far wrong. And though my heart's desire was three thousand miles away, her fax awaited me. Sadly so did my mother, home before us courtesy of Railtrack.

'Wallis is having a nap,' she answered to my unspoken question as I walked through the door. She then proceeded to ignore me and started flapping over AnnaMaria, much to her consternation. At that point I knew she knew.

Not for the first time I considered matricide, but for the first time I realised that an offspring from AnnaMaria, whom my mother loved dearly, was the nearest she'd get to being a grandmother.

So I left her to it.

I read Anne's fax in the privacy of the bath. I'd already checked up on Wallis. Snoring through adenoids that would probably have to come out one day, she looked exhausted and peaceful. Her new shoes and a set of new clothes (Mum again) were placed neatly at the bottom of the bed. Another wave of feelings flooded me and I retreated to the pine-scented bathroom to read Anne's three-page missal.

I cried till there was nothing left.

Chapter 10

The days that followed were calmer and, apart from Wallis' presence, I stuck with my usual routine. As far as AnnaMaria's pregnancy was concerned, the cat was out of the bag and the folded buggy became a permanent fixture in the hallway, next to Laura's bike.

Fortunately, we didn't have to put up with my mother's flapping for long. She returned home the following day but promised regular visits. The only person sorry to see her go was Wallis.

AnnaMaria took a few days off work. She had an oil change to do and her Mondeo was chalked in for the weekend. Everything else could wait, including my Land-Rover.

Our unexpected day out had caused some discussion. There were still question marks over the proposed bypass. AnnaMaria's strange interaction with Sapphire bothered me somehow, though I'd not broached the subject. If she wanted to confide in me, she would. She wasn't the sort of person you could push. We also had the return of Laura and Gran looming in the distance, and Julia's growing interest in Ms Joshi occupied her every waking thought. Unfortunately, it occupied our every waking thought too, for when Julia went for someone in a big way her extended family went with her.

AnnaMaria found the Saturday supplement she'd mentioned and I took time out to read about Sita Joshi one quiet afternoon when I had the house to myself. Julia had gone to work, AnnaMaria was spending time with her boyfriend, mainly to see how bruised his ego was, and Wallis was in the yard torturing the chickens. The odd squawk reassured me that they were still alive.

Before I settled down with the magazine, I reread Anne's fax. I'd almost memorised it, yet still it brought a lump to my throat.

I'd managed a short reply to a c/o address in New York, but I still wasn't entirely sure where she was stopping yet. I got the distinct impression that my fax would chase her across the East Coast, the Midwest and California before it finally caught up with her. It was clear from her correspondence that her whirlwind tour of America was to be just that. There was no point in me trying to phone her (though BT had fixed the phone lines). She would contact me when she could. She swore that if she heard my voice she'd be on the next plane home. Sounded all right to me. I felt alternating twinges of jealousy and loneliness that a week ago I would have had time to dwell on. Now I barely had time to think.

AnnaMaria managed a PS to my random description of events and lovey-slushy stuff. I'd persuaded her that 'I'm pregnant, love AnnaMaria' wouldn't do, so she'd couched it in gentler terms. AnnaMaria figured out how the machine worked and the paper disappeared for a second with a beep. Anne had a couple of big city stopovers before she hit San Francisco, so I didn't expect to hear from her for a while.

The newspaper article on Sita Joshi was a revelation. AnnaMaria's remark that the MP was controversial was like saying the Beatles were marginally successful.

Sita Joshi had been born and educated in England, in Yorkshire in fact, and had obtained a first in Fine Arts at Leeds University. She had returned to her parents' birthplace, Bombay, to pursue a career in the film industry. There was little work for women in British film-making at that time – and, from what I can gather, there's not a fat lot now. The *Guardian* described her as 'gifted, a feminist whose work behind the camera was a radical departure from mainstream Asian cinema'. You know how the *Guardian* goes on. Supported financially by her wealthy and prominently placed family, she stepped neatly into the role of mentor to other less fortunate colleagues. The *Guardian* was right, it was a radical move. Films were made that would never normally have seen the light of day. Apparently they were much acclaimed, though as I'm a fan of the likes of *Terminator 2* and the noir *Bound*, Sita Joshi's arthouse films, so described in the paper, would never have had me rushing to buy a ticket. In the East, particularly, her style of direction and her support for young film-makers brought her deserved recognition. Her promising career, however, was brought to a crashing end when news of her private life was leaked to the press. The *Guardian* in its wisdom chose not to delve too deeply into Sita's background, but it didn't take much imagination to realise what had happened. She was a dyke in a conservative part of the world and a woman in a male-dominated industry. Sooner or later the two worlds were going to collide. Or so AnnaMaria assured me (in case I didn't catch the drift) in a handwritten note at the end of the article. The article, however, did explore Sita's next career move. Leaving the film industry behind, she took off to Australia, leasing land and renovating a property in a remote part of New South Wales. The *Guardian* again:

For some years now it has been a centre for women adventurers, a base for exploring the region's dangerous territories, and Ms Joshi spends several weeks a year there, indulging in her love of pot-holing and climbing. An interest in the Green movement eventually took her to Holland, where her involvement in politics brought her once more into the public eye. She maintains close links, even now, with Greenpeace.

I skimmed the following couple of paragraphs. It wasn't really her whale-saving activities that interested me.

The next bit caught my eye: 'It was during this time that she renewed her acquaintance with Kim Stove, the legendary performer and activist. They were the perfect radical couple. Now separated, Sita Joshi still speaks of Stove with fondness and, I felt, some regret.' Julia would be thrilled to read that.

The bulk of the article was made up of an in-depth interview with the woman that normally I would have saved for bed, easier to prepare than cocoa, but I trudged through most of it and discovered that her British political career had begun only recently, first as a councillor for Manchester and lately as an MP. She specialised in women's issues and environmental problems.

She had been catapulted into the limelight by, unusually for a prominent figure, well-publicised death threats that turned into a real attempt on her life when her car was blown up. Apparently she'd made some powerful enemies. Not just the usual motley crew of the religious right, who hated her because she was neither white, Christian nor straight, and big-business fat cats, but even former colleagues in the entertainment business. Her last film, a controversial short, was apparently a final slap in the mouth to the male-dominated Bollywood hierarchy.

Politically, she was seen as a bit of a Blairite, and to be fair, considering his fear of controversy, the man himself had taken a risk in supporting her candidacy, though she appeared to me to be the right person to have on your side should a bypass threaten.

I would have thought that her natural affinity would be with the Green Party, except they were never going to get into power. It would take more than a bit of global warming to dislodge the main parties and, succumbing to my usual cynicism where political figures were concerned, it seemed to me that the ambitious Ms Joshi couldn't wait for that.

No one had admitted responsibility for the bomb. There were the usual assumptions concerning Irish terrorists, though as far as I was aware ecology and sexual politics had never been at the top of their agenda.

A small device, the bomb could have easily been made by someone with GCSE chemistry and access to the Internet. Miraculously no one was hurt, but it had frightened Ms Joshi's entourage, if not the woman herself, though she'd since stepped up security – hence, I presumed, Sapphire and her heavyweight pal. Things had calmed down since then.

There was a stunning picture of Sita Joshi to accompany the article: black hair cut short, Armani suit hanging well on her statuesque form. Looking forty but probably nearer fifty, her half-smiling face and flashing brown eyes hid a world of experience. Julia's bachelor days were definitely numbered.

I suddenly realised she was our first 'out' lesbian MP. My, how times change. I was all the more determined to meet her, even though Julia would think I'd only show her up.

In conclusion, the reporter demanded that 'we watch this space, Sita Joshi's star is in the ascendance'.

AnnaMaria had added further comments in the margins: 'Letty, you should follow the news more. A woman of your age has no excuse for not knowing what's going on.'

Well, pardon me! And who was she to talk? *The Times* Correspondent of the Year?

I ripped the relevant page out and wrote a short covering note to Anne: 'Guess who Julia's seeing!' I remembered AnnaMaria's instructions on how to use the fax machine and watched as it busily ate the page before spitting it out again. High-tech suddenly had its uses. I'd never have got round to posting the thing.

Chapter 11

The first signs of an impending disaster came the following Thursday, though I was probably the last to realise.

We had a particularly wet and windy day, too wet even for Wallis. She'd trailed sludgy water into the kitchen and had insisted on making lunch for everyone.

AnnaMaria, working three days a week for the moment, was in the attic, transforming it into living quarters. Andy was helping her, having forgiven her her transgressions with the mystery man. Smitten, he'd have forgiven an assassination attempt on the Pope. There was no talk of them living together, but having clapped eyes on the attic, AnnaMaria knew a good thing when she saw one.

And finally Julia was expected at one o clock with the lovely Sita.

'She'll have to take us as she finds us.' I'd found myself muttering my mother's words when Julia dropped the news on me. Though of course I'd spent hours cleaning the house. Even the chickens had had a wash and brush up.

'I'll make the sandwiches,' Wallis pronounced.

Perched on a stool over the worktop, she looked like an extra from *Ready Steady, Cook*. My one apron reached her ankles and a teacloth kept her hair out of her eyes. I'd also found a plastic knife to reduce the risk of her opening a vein.

The morning's foray into the village had produced enough consumables for a cricket tea and Wallis was surrounded by Warburton's soft white sliced bread, veg pâté, sliced hard-boiled eggs, fish paste (for those with a less discerning palate), cheese and mounds of chopped salad. I'd pushed the boat out and made my own recipe mushroom soup, rejecting my first idea of a curry. Sita might be a McDonald's fan for all I knew. It wasn't exactly a gourmet meal but one Wallis would enjoy preparing. It also took her mind off the imminent arrival of her gran and Laura, due the following day.

I'd had a letter from them at the weekend confirming the date of their return. It was obvious why she'd not rung to tell me. She probably thought I'd go mad. Actually, her main problems would be with AnnaMaria. With motherhood not so very far away, she wanted to strangle her.

My written version to Anne had fallen a bit short of the mark. It was enough to say that her sister had arrived from Australia and would be staying a while. I decided to leave it to Laura to explain the rest.

One o'clock came and went, and by two I'd given up any hope of Julia and Sita appearing. Knowing Julia, she'd not been able to drag herself out of bed, such was Ms Joshi's appeal.

In the end I was forced to ring Julia.

'Sorry, sorry, sorry,' she said breathlessly. (I was beginning to think I was right about her sexual exertions.) 'Sita can't make it . . . family problems. It looks as though she might have to go to India. I'll get back to you. Bye.'

I didn't even have a chance to comment, so we ate the lunch anyway, even Wallis' curious sandwiches. While some were overloaded with filling, about every third sandwich had nothing in it at all. Not even butter. A couple were lettuce only, though I'd managed to extract two inventions of her own. I didn't know if the weeds she'd introduced were deadly or not, and they were certainly colourful, but if by chance my guests did appear, I didn't want Ms Joshi's promising career to be cut short, and I didn't want to be sued either. The last sandwich had everything in it, including a couple of errant chicken feathers.

What we couldn't manage we sent upstairs to Andy, who was varnishing the attic's wooden floors.

'I'm glad they didn't come,' AnnaMaria stated, ladling soup into a bowl for Wallis. 'I bet that Sita's a right stuck-up cow.'

'AnnaMaria!' I said, shocked. 'That's a bit strong.'

'Not really,' she said. 'She goes out with Julia, doesn't she?' She'd still not forgiven her for telling everyone she was pregnant.

'Well, I like her,' Wallis interrupted, ripping the crusts off her sandwiches.

'That's because she buys you presents,' AnnaMaria

reminded her.

'No, she doesn't,' Wallis replied flatly.

'What about that Action Man doll?'

'Not Julia,' she said. 'That other lady. She knew my mum.'

Scooping lettuce from her soup, Wallis commenced eating.

I looked across at AnnaMaria, who gave me a shrug. A very Julia shrug. They'd worked together too long.

'When?' I asked in surprise.

'I got the 'ages and ages ago' reply.

'Small world,' I said thoughtfully.

'Very,' AnnaMaria agreed.

Later, as we prepared for bed, our conversation turned to Wallis' cryptic comment.

'It would be in Australia of course,' AnnaMaria declared. 'When this Joshi woman lived there.'

'But that was years ago,' I protested.

'Yeah, well, apparently she still keeps a house there,' she reasoned.

'It's a big place, Australia.'

AnnaMaria laughed. 'Small world, though,' she said, throwing my words back at me.

'I suppose,' I agreed reluctantly.

'Lesbians, they're all the same,' AnnaMaria stated. 'It's like a worldwide network. You've either slept with them or you know someone who has.'

'I'm sorry,' I retorted. 'I don't know any of them.'

'Yeah, but you know Julia,' she said drily. 'And, let's face it, she's slept with everyone.'

I couldn't argue with that.

Chapter 12

To my relief, I missed Laura's arrival and the first I heard was AnnaMaria giving Wallis' guardian a firm piece of her mind.

We were returning from a field trip, Wallis and I, a recce into the rarely visited depths of the farm. A sizeable collection of young trees grew there, along with accompanying wildlife. A group of grey squirrels had recently taken up residence and we'd watched in awed silence as the female, preparing for spring and the arrival of her young, collected the last of winter's wrinkled berries and forayed for nuts buried the previous autumn.

It was a little after dawn and, apart from the odd screech from Erik, all was oh so quiet. The damp patch of woodland was a relatively recent addition to the farm. Andy and AnnaMaria had decided we needed a wooded area and they'd spent a whole summer planting saplings and trees as an environmental project. I don't know where they got their supplies but suspected the park in nearby Halifax was short of a few shrubs. The virginal woods were as full of nature's mysteries as an Amazon jungle. Well, I thought so anyway.

Wallis whooped with delight when she heard Laura's voice and she took off as fast as her little legs would carry her. She wasn't interested in reasons or excuses. She just had her Laura back and that was all that mattered.

I trailed behind, too full of missing Anne to get into a fight. AnnaMaria was better at it than me. I always lost my train of thought at the crucial moment. You know, when your opponent is in a corner, on the verge of admitting that, whatever it was, it was their fault all along. And then my mind goes blank. Never fails.

'You lack the killer instinct,' Julia had admonished years ago. I found I could live without it.

I stood by the chicken run and watched the woman and the little girl greet each other. AnnaMaria had thrown her hands skywards in despair before stomping back into the kitchen. Both Laura and Wallis were crying. There was no pretence at emotions, it was all quite real. Laura's van was parked on the driveway, its engine ticking quietly. There was no sign of Gran. In fact, there was no sign of anyone else. Where were the troops she'd promised?

I trudged over to them after giving them a moment and Laura looked at me, tear-filled eyes rather wary.

'Don't worry,' I said. 'AnnaMaria's shouted at you for both of us.'

'I'm sorry, Letty,' she began.

I waved her to silence. I was getting good at that. 'Are you on your own?' I asked.

'For the moment,' she said, hugging Wallis. 'I would have been back earlier, but Gran's had to go into hospital.'

'God, why?' I asked. I'd only met the older woman once and her health, while obviously poor, hadn't looked that bad.

'Pneumonia. I promised Wallis we'd visit.'

'Will she be okay?' I asked, beckoning the pair indoors.

'Looks like she'll be in for a while.'

We clattered into the kitchen and Laura sat precariously on the edge of a stool, Wallis sprawled across her knee, clinging to her in case she slipped away again. Poor little soul, she'd missed her far more than she'd let on.

'Have you heard from Anne?' Laura asked tentatively as I made coffee, having abandoned the teapot for a more immediate hit.

'I've had a fax but I've not spoken to her. To be honest, I don't know where she is at the moment. I've written to her to let her know you're here, but whether she's received it or not . . .' I paused, juggling mugs.

I turned to find Laura nervously chewing her thumbnail. I passed her a coffee.

'Are you okay?'

'What? Oh, yes. Sorry, I'm fine. It's just been a bit hectic. I did try to ring you, but at first the phone wasn't working and then I couldn't catch you in.'

'The snow affected the lines again,' I explained. 'So what are your plans now?'

I took a seat opposite her.

'Well, I've managed to get a group of friends together. Friends we've known in the past. You'd be surprised where they turn up.'

Wallis squirmed on her knee at the news and sat up excitedly.

'Talking of knowing people,' I began, 'Julia – you know, the woman you met here?'

Laura nodded and sipped her coffee.

'She's seeing a woman Wallis seems to know. Sita Joshi? Apparently she was a friend of Wallis' mum.'

Laura's face was suddenly set and unfathomable. She shrugged her shoulders.

'From Australia?' I pressed on.

'Don't know the name,' she muttered.

'You know,' Wallis chimed in. 'That Indian lady.'

'I must have forgotten,' she replied, ruffling Wallis' hair.

I got the impression that the subject was definitely closed.

'Thanks for getting Wallis some clothes,' Laura said, examining the child's new outfit.

I took the hint. 'My mother bought them. She can't resist kids.'

'Oh, yes, I meant to ask,' Laura went on. 'Who's the buggy for?'

I pointed upstairs. 'AnnaMaria, mother-to-be. That's partly why you got it in the neck.'

'I don't blame her,' Laura said, finishing her coffee. 'It did look like I'd deserted Wallis. And on that point, I wonder if I could impose on you a bit longer.'

I hesitated. I'd been put upon enough.

'Just until this bypass is sorted. If I could use your farm as a base. The others are staying on site at Batley Close, near where the new road is supposed to start.'

'I thought it hadn't been decided yet. There's to be a

meeting in Calderton soon. Ms Joshi's chairing it.' I waited for a reaction. There was none. 'Anyway, Batley Close is where Julia's garage is situated. She'd know about it, surely.'

Under normal circumstances what Julia should know and what she did know weren't necessarily one and the same thing. But Sita Joshi must have had some idea and, rightly or wrongly, would have informed Julia. What was the point in knowing (or, in this case, sleeping with) people in high places if they couldn't help?

As if on cue, the phone rang. It was Julia, resurfacing after an unexplained absence. I knew what she was going to say even before she said it.

'Letty, what the bloody hell's going on?' she exploded. 'There are tents and metal objects and sodding vans all over the road.'

I held the phone away from my ear as she ranted, though George could probably hear her next door.

'And they all look like that bloody Laura. What's going on?' she yelled again.

To anyone else it would be obvious.

'It's those bloody tree people, isn't it?' she bellowed, as light dawned.

'I thought you wanted their help?' I asked.

'Oh, no,' she said, exasperated. 'We don't even know what's happening yet and when we do we'll protest through the council, and the courts if we have to. I'm not having this lot on my land.'

Julia, her true conservative nature to the fore, was suddenly knowledgeable about local politics.

'Julia, calm down,' I snapped, fed up with her.

Another voice suddenly crackled across the airwaves.

AnnaMaria from the upstairs extension.

'I've got a say in this, remember,' she growled. 'Anyway, she's frightened it'll damage her girlfriend's career,' she added with some malice.

'Sita's not even in the country,' Julia replied curtly.

'Hah!' AnnaMaria snorted and slammed the phone down.

It took a moment for my hearing to recover.

'Since when?' I said, head reeling.

'Since when what?'

'God, Julia, since when has she been out of the country?'

'I'll tell you tonight. I'll be around about six. I'll stay at yours, if that's okay. I want to be at the garage early tomorrow. Look, I've got to go. Bye, Letty.'

'I'm going to the Kim Stove concert tonight,' I said to a dead phone. I tried to ring her back but she'd switched her mobile off.

'Did you hear any of that?' I asked Laura, retrieving my coffee.

It was stone cold, so I chucked it down the sink.

'Couldn't miss it really,' she said with a smile.

I found myself looking at Anne's face. It was uncanny. Despite the age difference, they were so alike.

'It's a legitimate protest,' Laura insisted, rolling a cigarette. 'And if Julia thinks she can change anything another way, she's mistaken.'

Laura was calmer, on firmer ground, and her arguments were very convincing. Especially to someone like me, who was ignorant of the whole process.

'What do you need my field for? Why won't you be staying at the . . . I groped for the right word.

'Camp?' she offered.

I nodded.

'Not with Wallis. It's not very healthy for her. It can be dangerous at times too,' she added darkly.

She faltered then, wondering, I was sure, whether to tell me more. For some reason, she decided against it.

'You've seen the van. We can live well in that, but still stage our protest. Wallis can learn a lot from this.' And she hugged the child again.

I was tempted to ask her about Wallis' schooling. She was a bright kid and I found it hard to believe she'd not had some sort of formal education. Still the three Rs aren't everything. Perhaps she *could* learn enough on the road.

'How long will it take?' I asked tentatively.

'To be honest, if things aren't resolved in the first few weeks, you know you've lost. The media lose interest. The locals are sick of seeing us. Look at Julia, and we haven't been there twenty-four hours yet.'

'Don't worry about Julia,' AnnaMaria said from the hallway, having taken a break from decorating. 'That garage is half mine, remember.'

Great, something else for them to argue about.

Laura smiled at the unexpected support. AnnaMaria had obviously overcome her disgust at the other woman's conduct.

Laura went on, 'Unless you can come up with something extraordinary after that, you've had it.'

'So what happens now?' I asked again.

'First, you haven't answered my question,' she reminded gently. 'Can we stay?'

I remembered the last time someone had had free

94

access to my land – disastrous doesn't begin to describe it but then I thought of Anne and then I thought of Wallis and then I said yes. She breathed a long, slow sigh of relief. 'I can't thank you enough.'

In retrospect she was right. She couldn't.

Chapter 13

It wasn't my first trip to the Apollo by any means. My visits had been intermittent since the very early eighties when, as a folk aficionado, I'd caught every concert Steeleye Span had ever given. My tastes in music, like Julia's in furnishings, had changed, though Anne, finding folk music a bit wet, still teased me about my hippie pretensions. So I only played my records when she was out. Sadly that would give me plenty of album time in the next couple of months.

Getting to the Stove concert at all had been an orgy of organisation. I'd nearly not bothered, until my mother turned up. That would drive anybody out.

But she hadn't just come to visit. My mother was hoping to do a deal with a ticket tout and so, in a typically complicated Letty Campbell sort of way, we all ended up going to Manchester together. I had Julia's spare keys, so with no return journey guaranteed, at least we had somewhere to sleep. I didn't want to drive, hoping for a drink later, and all AnnaMaria could manage was her motorbike; not in my wildest imaginings could I see myself on the back of that with a pregnant woman. So it was Mum and her BMW or nothing. We'd get a train back in the morning.

I put a note on the table for Julia (she still had keys to the farm and would have had no qualms about letting herself in), explaining my movements. I didn't want her to think she'd had burglars in her absence. You could never be too sure after a visit from AnnaMaria.

As usual, my last task was to feed the chickens, and while I'd finally worked out how to use the automatic feeder that I'd found in the back of the garage, Erik, chief and elder of the tribe, liked the personal touch. He also liked giving me the odd nip and I chased him for a bit, clapping my hands, until he conceded defeat. He stalked off, shaking his feathers, and I retrieved a couple that had fallen loose, intending to add them to Wallis' growing collection. I was surprised how much I missed her: her unintentional wit, her affection, even her interminable questions. I locked the chickens up for the night and tried not to dwell on my feelings.

Mum mithered me into hurrying. 'Are you ready, dear?' she asked, looking me up and down.

'Surely these jeans will do?' I sighed.

It was hard to believe we were dressed in similar clothes. My jeans were faded but clean and my T-shirt was an anonymous white affair.

Mum's denims were classic-cut Western style, off the peg M&S, white T-shirt again, with a little frilly lace effect around the neck. She'd ironed a crease in the jeans. She was top-and-tailed by Le Coq white anorak (with a navy flash) and matching blue and white Le Coq trainers. Where, I wanted to know, was the tennis racquet?

AnnaMaria steered me outside, the only non-lesbian I knew who wore dungarees. In fact the only person – period.

'Don't get into a fight with Margaret,' she said and laughed, having heard my comment even if Mum hadn't. 'Do you know how many dodgy characters she'll have to approach to get a ticket? The poor woman's stressed enough.' She shoved me into the back of the car. 'Anyway, life's too short.'

She ran back down the yard and locked up the house before making herself comfortable in the car.

I'd still not heard any of Kim Stove's music, art or whatever it was, and the tape Mum had brought along became a victim of the BMW's voracious appetite. The cassette player chewed it up.

'Never mind, Letitia,' Mum said, burning rubber down the motorway. 'It'll be a nice surprise.'

It was a surprise all right.

Two thousand lesbians and three gay men were already at the Apollo when we arrived.

A rainbow of hormones hovered over the stage. I'd won tickets for a k d lang concert once and the atmosphere there had been similar but less international. This was like the Five Nations Cup.

I went berserk and paid six quid for a programme. According to the bumph, this was the third of only six worldwide concerts she was doing this year. If she could pack 'em, rack 'em and stack 'em like she did at this concert, then I was naturally curious as to why her concerts were so rare and why she picked Manchester over, say, Munich or Milan, Newark over New York, Seattle over Sydney, but I was no wiser after reading the piece.

It started off quite well in an arty type of way: 'I draw strength and inspiration from my lovers. The air they breathe, the space they use – ' I started to lose interest here – 'is as important to me as my own space, my own breath.'

The next sentence brought me back with a bang:

'And for every womanlover that has shared my bed-space or a moment in my life, that special affinity is reflected in my work. Every movement, every song has a woman's inspirational touch.'

I looked at the footnote to the pamphlet. She had a ninety-minute set. How many women did you have to sleep with to be inspired for ninety minutes? She went on in a similar vein, though her words became increasingly sensuous, bordering on an eroticism that had somehow escaped the censor's hand. Not surprisingly, the well-lit hall was almost silent as the crowd read these strange, almost disconcerting ramblings.

Even Mum, having successfully secured a ticket, a T-shirt and a programme, was lost to the verse, a slight smile on her lips.

As the artist blathered on, I was more than ready to hate her.

AnnaMaria was watching me, grinning at my reaction rather than Kim Stove's words.

'What a load of old crap,' I whispered.

A quickly smothered bellow of laughter answered me,

though an irritated shuffle of feet from somewhere nearby reminded us we were shortly to be in the company of greatness.

The atmosphere, as the countdown to the artist's appearance grew closer, became more nuclear fission than electric, more Prince Nazeem than Prince, more George Best than George Elliot. I almost expected the young dyke in front of me, already dressed in a Stove T-shirt, to spontaneously combust, she was in such a state.

We were plunged from bright light to pitch black in a moment and the audience, me included, took a collective breath.

We were left in this darkness (even the safety lights had been extinguished) for several moments until a ray of light appeared from the stage. Dodging and darting among the audience, a face was suddenly traced out in all its ghostly monochrome glory. Another light appeared, picking faces at random, and then another, and on and on until lights streamed across the whole audience, the watchers becoming players. Ever practical, I hoped no one in the crowd was epileptic.

Despite myself, I couldn't help but feel that what followed was one of the most extraordinary events I had ever witnessed. I could see why the place was packed, and though Oasis had no immediate worries about being shoved from the Number One slot, Kim Stove's set was a very rare phenomenon indeed. As was the woman herself.

Born in Holland to a Persian mother and a Dutch father, she had a dark and dangerous beauty that, according to AnnaMaria, *Vogue* had been trying to sign up for years.

Her singsong, doo-be-doo accent was American-influenced and all the more charming for that, and it was an instrument she wasn't afraid to use to entice her already infatuated audience.

Her music had an international feel to it and only some of the more traditional sounds appealed to me. But there was much more to her than that. She introduced me to a world of dance and colour, and a stage show of such spectacular warmth and vibrancy that the narrow confines of the Apollo could barely contain. I half expected her to lead the spectators from the auditorium and take them on a merry dance through the streets of Manchester. The scary thing is, most of them would have followed too. By the end of her act, so would I.

Her entrance was unforgettable, a joy to watch. Backlit by lights representing fire, her black-clad figure appeared above a cleverly disguised staircase. It was almost as if it was suspended among billowing clouds of smoke and sparks. The music accompanying her dance made the soundtrack from *Death in Venice* seem almost banal. It was as though a dozen orchestras were grappling for first shot at the music. Almost from that moment we knew we were to be participants in, and not merely spectators of, her rapturous collection of music and art.

The first part of her act was dedicated to the four elements and, with support from a young Slovenian dance troupe, the performance didn't have the twee overtones I'd been dreading. The fire and air sequences were followed by earth, from primeval eruptions to the quakes and shakes of a turn-of-the-century San Francisco. Lights, dance and music brought it all to life, even bewitching an old cynic like me. The final part of this first act was dedicated to the element of water, and the delicately undulating music and shadowy dance movements invoked the warm and gentle pull of the Mediterranean. I could almost feel it lap softly around my toes.

We had a two-minute break, just enough to get our breath back, before the second of her three-part stage act was revealed. Pummelled by her portrayal of the elements, we were brought to the private place of her poetry. It was the bit I'd been dreading. The stuff that usually made me cringe was laid out for me to examine.

It was an amazing experience, and it turned my own prejudices on their head. Thunderous roars of passion were delivered unaccompanied by music, and from there we were led to safe harbours where her love poetry was quietly directed to sisters, mothers, lovers. And then somehow I almost began to see the point. Her words weren't directed to the audience, they were marked for me, and though I didn't entirely understand the nuances, I knew it was personal.

But for me the highlight of the evening was her final set. She'd saved the best till last and the selection of Persian love songs needed a three-pack of Kleenex.

Choosing to use a simple background – sheets of grey silk billowing gently behind her – she took a seat at the front of the stage. Accompanying herself with first an acoustic guitar and then a dulcimer, its delicate silver strings reminding me somehow of cowbells, she sang songs of such heartbreaking sadness I almost couldn't bear it. The pain of missing Anne was a live thing crawling under my skin as Kim's words enveloped me. Only the final number stopped me sobbing aloud.

'My last song tonight,' she said, that gloriously deep

voice rising above the applause, 'is a song from the village of my mother's ancestors.' She paused to smile at the panting spectators. 'I've taken the liberty of adding a Dutch flavour. I think you'll like it,' she assured us. At that point she could have recited the Bible backwards and still have brought the roof down.

Now, I wouldn't know a Dutch musical flavour if it launched itself out of a tulip and hit me in the face, and when she'd finished the song I still couldn't pick out the European influences, but that didn't stop me loving it, though.

Most of the audience were on their feet, stamping and clapping, with enough whistling and jigging for a Saw Doctors' tour. I caught sight of Mum bop-bopping down the aisle, a teenager on one arm and a woman old enough to be my gran on the other.

Kim Stove's performance had obvious appeal to the lesbians who made up a large proportion of the audience, but her attraction was more widespread than that. Mum was the tip of the iceberg as far as I could see. The artist would appeal to any sexuality, any age, anyone who could suspend their own preconceived ideas about performance art. She appealed, in fact, to someone like me.

The effect, and even the memory of the effect, only stopped hours after she had ended her ninety-minute set. I was left shaken, and the combined efforts of the audience to bring the woman back on for an encore were stunning. Anne would have loved her, I thought sadly.

AnnaMaria hauled me to my feet. 'She doesn't do encores,' she insisted as we staggered from the auditorium.

The frustrated audience, denied a second glance at their idol, twitched its way out in our wake. I could imagine long, steamy nights ahead for some of them, such was the sexual tension in the air. I had no idea what effect it had had on Mum, and to be honest I didn't want to know, but she was very cheerful.

'Well, what did you think?' she asked as we clambered back into the car (an eight-year-old local hoodlum had done a good job of protecting the vehicle, three pounds well spent).

'Different,' I agreed, still reeling from the effects, both special and personal. 'Not quite what I expected. Anyway, how come you never mentioned her before?'

How come I'd never heard of her before, come to that?

Mum laughed and started the car. 'I did. You switched off when I mentioned "Performance Artist".'

I smiled and reached behind me for the seat belt. A mad and pierced face suddenly loomed at me through the window. Sapphire, grinning.

My heart missed a beat in shock. I couldn't stand much more of this.

'Hold on, Margaret,' I ordered Mum, winding the window down.

'Hiya,' Sapphire greeted us, unconcerned. 'I thought I saw you at the concert. Brilliant, wasn't she?'

Vigorous nods all round.

'Are you going on anywhere?' she asked.

'Any suggestions?' AnnaMaria, suddenly enthusiastic, wanted to know.

'The Factory's open till three. Women-only upstairs if anyone's interested. You'll have to look sharp, though. That's where everybody's headed.'

The Factory was the latest haunt for gay babes, and a babe I was not. It wasn't a label that hung comfortably with any of us, and AnnaMaria, dungaree-clad, would probably get arrested by the fashion police. Mum would hate it.

'Oh, I'll try that,' Mum enthused. 'Is it far?'

'Just off Oxford Road,' Sapphire explained. 'Can I beg a lift if you're going?"

'Of course,' Mum said.

I moved over to let Sapphire in. My elbow brushed her ribs. She had no gun this time, thank God.

'Have we met?' Mum asked, crashing the gears.

'Well, not actually met,' Sapphire replied.

I could see her dark and serious profile in the half-light of the car's interior. The woman really did have to lighten up a bit. She was a different person to the young radical I had known.

'I work for Ms Joshi. I saw you at the Green Rooms recently.'

'Oh,' Mum said, embarrassed. She prided herself on her memory. 'I remember now.'

'Aren't you working tonight, then?' I asked as Mum eased her way into the traffic.

'No,' Sapphire replied, settling herself. 'Ms Joshi's away.'

'Oh, yes. I'd thought she might have been at the concert, being a friend of Kim Stove's, but Julia told me she was abroad,' I said, probing as I remembered my friend's words.

Sapphire, as evasive as ever, chose not to elaborate.

She was right about the Factory. The whole of the Apollo

was headed in the same direction. Mum drove like a maniac and, with Sapphire's streetwise instructions, we got there ahead of the throng.

We had no problem getting into the place. We all looked like lesbians, even if most of us weren't. I was worried there might have been a hiccup when Mum tried to get over the threshold, but the doorwoman took a look at those sensible shoes and she was in. Personally I couldn't fathom out the double standards. You were only supposed to get in if you were gay and yet there was an odd sort of disapproval if you looked like a dyke. Designer club wear was fine, it didn't matter how naff it was. But some smart dykey suit broke all the unwritten rules of the club. Sister George wouldn't have lasted five minutes.

In some strange way Mum was flattered. It seemed best not to question her.

It's not very often I'm tempted with drugs (discounting alcohol) but on this occasion I would have happily dropped a couple of slimming tablets. I couldn't talk – one of my favourite occupations – over the boom of the music, I couldn't dance and missing Anne would kick in again soon. I could drink, though, and the ice-cold Bud was heavenly.

Mum had no problem doing all three, except she was drawn to the Slush Puppies on sale rather than the booze. I don't think she realised the iced soft drink was there as an alternative to water when the designer drugs began to take effect.

Mum left, reluctantly, after an hour or so. She had a long drive ahead of her. Damp from her exertions, she gave me a peck on the cheek (Kim Stove really had had an effect), screamed in my ear, 'I'VE HAD A WONDERFUL TIME. RING ME,' and disappeared to retrace her steps to the car.

There were four seats in the club. AnnaMaria and Sapphire had one each and I took the third next to a corpse. The blonde, faceless creature was utterly still. There was no tell-tale sign of life, no rise and fall of her skinny, nylon-clad chest.

'Is it dead?' I asked a cider-swigging Sapphire.

She looked across to check. 'Is it warm? Does it have a pulse?' she yelled back.

The alcohol had finally loosened her up a bit.

'It must be ninety degrees in here! A three-day-old cadaver would still be warm in this place, probably still have a pulse too!' AnnaMaria roared.

Julia's dark humour was rubbing off.

I prodded the prone woman, not something I'd normally do sober. She grunted, proof enough that at least one cell was still functioning.

I made a last trip to the bar and, after a short and brutal battle through the crowds, returned to my chair, now occupied by another emaciated body. Why didn't they share a seat? There was plenty of room for two. My companions had vacated theirs, though, and as the music subtly changed to a gentler but still-insistent drum and bass beat, I cast around, trying to see if the pair of them were dancing.

Against any odds I would have cared to propose, I spotted Sapphire and AnnaMaria in a corner of the club, hands touching gently. There was a powerful air of intimacy between the two women that floored me, and I watched, too drunk for subtlety, as AnnaMaria reached up and softly stroked Sapphire's face. I was stunned – not because I'd always assumed AnnaMaria was straight, and frankly Sapphire's sexuality was unknown, but because I thought I knew the woman well enough.

Just goes to show, doesn't it?

Chapter 14

'So, she's a dyke, then?' I couldn't resist asking on the train home the following morning.

'I knew you were going to ask that,' AnnaMaria replied crossly.

Sapphire, not so surprisingly, had stayed the night at Julia's pad in Hulme. It could have been awkward, but I was drunk enough not to care. I'd passed out on the settee and the two women had retired to Julia's futon. Or at least I assumed they had. Sapphire had left before I woke up.

'Aren't you going to ask if I am?' AnnaMaria broke into my thoughts.

'Would you tell me?' I challenged.

There was a significant pause. 'Probably not,' she admitted. 'Anyway, she won't sleep with anyone unless there's some sort of commitment, or an ongoing relationship.'

'So she's not a lesbian, then?'

AnnaMaria gave me a look. I thought for a moment she wasn't going to speak to me at all, and then suddenly she grinned.

'Oh, Ms Cynic, what a nosy cow you are,' she stated flatly.

I grinned back. I couldn't deny it – my biggest fault.

The train began to slow down, its airbrakes sighing gently as we came into the station.

'Come on,' AnnaMaria said. 'We're home.'

It was a while before I found out the truth.

Chaos, Julia and panic were a well-known combination and this particular Saturday morning was no exception. We were paying a visit just to see how Julia was coping at the garage. The fact that she'd barricaded herself in said it all.

Despite the changeable weather, a carnival atmosphere surrounded the premises. Clowns, jugglers and women on stilts milled about. Colourfully dressed, there was no doubt that they were the travellers and road protesters Laura had promised. They were the other end of the spectrum to the visitors Julia and AnnaMaria usually had. There wasn't much danger of this lot trying to flog double-glazing.

Julia had put up a huge sign in the office window. 'WE ARE OPEN FOR BUSINESS' it optimistically read, though how a potential punter could get near the place was beyond me.

'Letty, AnnaMaria,' a voice called from the crowd.

I looked for a familiar face. Laura and Wallis appeared. The little girl crawled all over a delighted AnnaMaria and I got Laura's questions.

'Have you seen the camp?' she asked breathlessly. 'On Middleton Road. It's buzzing.'

'No,' I admitted. 'We've only just arrived.'

I glanced at the garage and Julia's pale and furious face appeared briefly in the office window. The door was flung open and she stormed out. In seconds Laura had grabbed Wallis and disappeared back into the cheerful rabble.

'Get away from those frigging cars!' Julia bellowed at a couple of kids who in truth were nowhere near them.

'Julia! In!' I ordered and frogmarched her back to the office with AnnaMaria, maliciously enjoying Julia's predicament, hot on my heels.

'Look,' I said after wrestling her into the single (still-broken) office chair, 'I don't know what your problem is. Once the protest gets going, it can only do you good. It's pointless waiting for your girlie to do something. This affects more than just you, you know.' My hangover was still hanging about and I was in no mood for Julia's tantrums. 'All this is a great publicity stunt. There are more photographers than protesters out there.'

Admittedly that was a bit of an exaggeration, but there had been a few cameras in evidence. Well, I'd spotted Janice, Mrs Buckham's niece, who was covering the story for the *Calderton Echo*, at any rate.

At the thought of free publicity, Julia bucked up a bit, but not entirely. Her main problems were of a more personal nature.

'It's Sita,' she said with a sigh.

'What's happened now?' AnnaMaria asked curtly.

'This,' Julia said, scrabbling in her briefcase. After a moment she produced a typed letter. 'Just read it.'

Tentatively I took Julia's place on the clapped-out chair.

'Dearest Julia,' it began, promisingly enough. 'I know

this will be difficult for you to understand.' Downhill immediately. 'And as much as I've enjoyed our time together, I feel I can't carry on seeing you. I could blame pressure of work. You know the sort of thing I am involved with – the bypass is one of many projects close to my heart. But this letter comes from a much more personal viewpoint and one I cannot clarify at the moment . . .'

I turned the page over. 'Where's the rest?' I asked, puzzled.

'That's it,' Julia sighed. 'She must have forgotten to put the other page in.'

'That's pathetic! How can you forget something like that?' AnnaMaria snapped, taking the letter from my hand. 'It doesn't make sense. Some sort of MP she is,' she muttered.

'I don't get it,' Julia said, hurt by the whole thing. 'It was going so well. And look at the date on the letter. That was the day we were supposed to come to yours for lunch. I've not seen her since then.' She paused. 'I thought she'd got over Kim,' she mumbled, half to herself.

AnnaMaria glanced in my direction. Julia's quiet comment made things a little clearer.

'So you think she's gone back to her?' I asked as gently as I could.

Julia shrugged. 'All I know is she's gone to India. Sapphire rang to tell me. There's no forwarding address and this half-letter had been pushed through the office door. And there are three hundred lunatics outside,' she added angrily as the noise beyond the office intensified. 'Oh, great,' she moaned, peering out of the window. 'The police have arrived now.'

'Well, any publicity is better than no publicity,' AnnaMaria pointed out.

Only Richard Nixon's statement 'There'll be no whitewash at the White House' was ever more wrong.

Chapter 15

Janice the photographer was ecstatic. You'd think she'd scooped the Pulitzer Prize, the way she was whooping and flashing. Her camera was alternately shoved in my mug and then in Julia's shocked and pale face.

'More film!' Janice screamed to her sixteen-year-old Work Experience assistant. She couldn't believe her luck. The peaceful protest that she'd been sent to cover had taken second place to the story unfolding before her. 'Take notes,' she yelled to the unfortunate school-leaver. 'Miss Rossi, have you a statement?' she bellowed to Julia. The camera flashed again.

'Janice, piss off,' I growled.

'Ms Campbell, have you anything to say?' she asked, turning to me. 'Do you know her? Were you involved? Was it a lesbian love triangle?"

There was a sudden mad flurry in the crowd and a fist buried itself in Janice's nose. Blood flew and Janice hit the deck. There was a short tussle over the camera and Janice, clinging to her moment of glory and her unexpected scoop, won the fight for its possession.

'AnnaMaria, leave her!' I ordered as the two women struggled on the floor.

A policeman, taken by surprise at the ferocity of the fight, managed to separate the two women. I waded in, more concerned about AnnaMaria's state of health than any photo.

Jostled by police and road protesters we were pushed to one side and were left to watch helplessly as Julia was bundled into the back of a waiting police car.

'Ring my mother!' were her last words before she disappeared from view.

If I had just been dragged off by the police, ringing my mother would be the last thing on my mind. Under the circumstances, surely a lawyer would have been more useful.

Not only had Sita Joshi failed to arrive at Bombay Airport, she'd also never made it out of England. Her car had been found abandoned on the approach road to Manchester Airport. Blood was splattered across the back seats. Julia had insisted to the police that she'd not seen Sita for days. That was before she started bawling. Everything was a bit of a jumble after that.

Some hotshot inspector from Manchester had his moment of glory with Julia's apprehension. The local bobby accompanying him had looked embarrassed. WPC Emma and Sergeant Sam were more used to sheep rustling and the odd teenage incident than this big-time stuff.

Janice was still on the floor, recovering from Anna-Maria's attack, when I approached her. She spotted

AnnaMaria and began crawling away.

'Janice, hang on,' I said. She clutched her camera tightly to her bosom, panic in her eyes. 'AnnaMaria,' I muttered, 'go and lock up the garage while I see that Janice is all right.'

'Huh,' she retorted, but made her way through the shocked crowds to secure the empty premises.

'This is going straight to my editor,' Janice insisted, holding the camera ever tighter as she got to her feet.

Janice and I were no strangers to each other and she was well known in the village too. Local girl made good, she had a flair for newspaper work and was busy dragging herself through a part-time photo-journalist course. Miraculously, she had secured a twenty-hour-a-week junior position on the local rag.

Janice loved Calderton and she had no plans to leave though like all journalists she hoped for the big story. Her aunt and most of her relatives still lived in these parts. Even her fiancé was a local lad. Mrs Buckham was a friend of mine and she'd told me enough about the young woman for me to know how her mind worked.

This story and these pictures would pay for the wedding. Work on the *Daily Express* didn't interest her; her needs were much simpler. Well, if she wanted to keep the camera and if she wanted AnnaMaria kept away from her, then she needed my co-operation.

I dabbed ineffectually at Janice's bloodied nose. She winced every time I went near her. I couldn't imagine her on a fact-finding mission with John Pilger somehow.

'What do you know about this?' I asked the bruised newswoman.

Not surprisingly, she was reluctant to tell me.

'Come on, Janice,' I implored. 'You must know something.'

AnnaMaria returned, looking disgruntled. 'Look? I'm sorry,' she snapped unconvincingly to the roving reporter. 'I was upset, that's all.'

'You're upset!' Janice retorted, brave now she could use me as a buffer. 'Do you know what this nose feels like? Anybody else would have you done for assault.'

I was worried that this had been her line of thinking. I had a feeling we'd be seeing enough of the police as it was, but if push came to shove I could put pressure on her aunt. Our egg contract had been going for years and she wouldn't want to lose it.

'Before we do anything rash,' I butted in, 'let's find out the facts. Nobody has really explained anything.'

AnnaMaria and I had been pushed out of the room before we could hear exactly what the police had on Julia. She may have had her moments (and her family's reputation was hardly squeaky clean), but for all her screaming and shouting, I couldn't imagine Julia being involved in anything really dodgy.

'WPC Emma's not saying much either,' AnnaMaria admitted. She glanced back to where the policewoman stood guard behind yards of crime-scene tape. 'Except that the forensic boys will be looking at the garage.'

God, were they mad? It would be simpler to split the atom than sift that dump for evidence.

'And we've got to be available if the police want to question us.'

'Oh, great,' I muttered.

Janice in the meantime was busily slipping rolls of film to her young assistant. 'Get these to John as quick as you can. They should make tonight's edition.'

The apprentice took off on foot. Janice followed this with a quick call on her mobile phone, presumably to John, her editor, advising him of the latest developments. She'd obviously decided to hang around to see if she could pick up any more information. Her ears were already flapping at the titbits she'd got from AnnaMaria.

Nose forgotten, she dragged her notebook from her pocket.

'Is there anything you want to tell me?' she asked, as subtle as a flying sledgehammer.

'Yeah,' AnnaMaria suggested. 'Stick to taking photos.'

'Look,' I said, 'we're not going to find out anything standing here, are we? If Sita's disappeared . . .' The thought made me shudder. The fact that I'd nearly said 'dead' made me want to throw up. 'Then it should be on the lunchtime news. Come on, let's get home.'

I looked around for means of transport. The cars on AnnaMaria's courtyard were obviously out of bounds. It was a three-mile walk home and taxis in Calderton were a bit thin on the ground at the best of times. I thought of Laura, but she was nowhere to be seen, even though the tree people, protest forgotten in the excitement of these unexpected events, were still milling about.

'I'll make you a deal,' Janice offered.

'Tell you what, I'll make you one,' AnnaMaria growled, ditching any attempts at contrition. 'Fuck off now and I won't rip your ears off.'

Janice took an alarmed step backwards. Unbeknown to Janice and for reasons known only to herself, reporters were on AnnaMaria's long list of scumbags.

Looking at AnnaMaria's furious face, I might have

suspected that the police had arrested the wrong woman had I not been able to account for every second of AnnaMaria's movements lately.

Janice turned to me. 'I'll get you home if you give me an exclusive.'

Janice had been watching way too many films, but I agreed to her terms. After all, the best I could do was give her exclusively nothing.

The midday news programme was full of it. They knew far more about events than I did and even Janice was hooked.

The stern-faced and delectable newsreader took us carefully through each incident. The woman's cool reporting summed it all up.

'In the early hours of this morning, the car of Sita Joshi, the controversial Member of Parliament for CalderVale, was discovered empty on the approach road to Manchester's Ringway Airport. Police say a quantity of blood was found in the vehicle, giving rise to concern over the well-being of the MP.'

A picture of Sita's Daimler appeared on the screen, surrounded by the now familiar blue and white tape. Despite the tea clutched in my hand, I was bone cold. The newsreader went on:

'Ms Joshi had already received death threats and had only recently survived a terrorist bomb attack on her car.'

Another picture flashed on the TV, this time a burnt-out hulk of a vehicle outside her home (prior to her move to Hulme) in Northenden.

'Although there has been no word as to why the MP had been targeted in such a way, sources say her support for Green issues may have led to today's events.'

She paused for a moment:

'News just in suggests a woman is being held for questioning. Sue Johnstone reports.'

The images got worse and we were passed over to a granite-voiced Sue, sporting her best 'Don't fuck with me' look, reporting outside Bootle Street Police Station. Well, at least I knew where Julia was.

'The woman detained this morning has been described as Sita Joshi's former lover. . .'

My feelings of nausea got worse.

'And although we are not allowed to give her name for legal reasons . . .'

'That won't stop John,' Janice muttered.

. . . we do know she is being held pending further investigations. The police have promised to make a statement later today. This is Sue Johnstone reporting for the BBC, Manchester.'

*

Back in the studio, the anchorwoman was joined by Tony Blair's deputy. Wearing black and looking solemn, he denounced the use of terror tactics in British politics. He admitted that at this time it was unclear whether Sita's disappearance was due to events of a more personal nature (cleverly avoiding 'gay' or 'lesbian' in his wording) or if she had been the victim of a political assault, making the assumption that the two couldn't be linked.

This was no help to me. In fact, the issue became more clouded by the second. I'd bet my life that Julia wasn't involved. The idea was too crazy to contemplate. How, when and why were only three of the questions that immediately came to mind. While upset at being dumped, Julia's libido had amazing powers of recovery, and it wouldn't be long before she was back on the happy sex trail again. As for politics – she was about as political as a goldfish.

Janice was busily scribbling in her notebook. I'd not said a word to her and AnnaMaria had hissed through the whole news broadcast. Finally Janice took the hint and cleared off back to her office at the *Echo*. Her fifteen minutes of fame were surely upon her.

AnnaMaria switched the telly off, not only mad but clearly upset too. For all their rows and bad-tempered bickering, she was as fond of Julia as I was.

'That's just crap,' she snapped. 'What do they think Julia is? A murderer? Please!'

God, as if I didn't have enough on my plate. I had to tell Anne. I had to tell someone. Julia's mother! I'd almost forgotten.

'AnnaMaria, where's Julia's emergency address list.

You know, the one with her mother's number on it?' I started to flap around the lounge.

'Sooner you than me,' she muttered, knowing the sort of response a call like this would get. 'Under the phone, where it always is.'

I took a deep breath and dialled the long-distance number.

Now, I don't know any Italian. None. Sadly, I was typically English where foreign languages were concerned and like a lot of my compatriots I have a mental blank beyond 'Two beers please.' So the conversation I had with Mrs Rossi's maid was like something from a Pink Panther film, but without the laughs.

AnnaMaria was no help. Even though she knew some Italian, she refused to impart this devastating information to Julia's mother.

Eventually the maid gave up on me and I was left for long moments with a silent phone. Before I was tempted to hang up, I heard the steady tread of high-heeled shoes on marble floors.

'*Si?*' Sophia Rossi enquired.

Well, at least I understood that much.

'Mrs Rossi, this is Letty Campbell here, from England,' I added stupidly. 'Your daughter's friend.'

'Letty! Of course, how are you? How wonderful to hear your voice. And how is your mother? Well, I hope?'

'Fine, fine,' I said, caught in polite conversation.

In the background, in the expensive luxury of the Milanese suburbs, I heard her call, 'Enrico, it is Letty, Julia's friend from England.'

She said this in English for my benefit, knowing how I

struggled with languages. Enrico had no such qualms and he prattled away in Italian. I caught '*Bambino*' and 'Julia' a couple of times. Oh, Daddy was going to be thrilled.

After we'd checked on each other's health for a while, I managed to get my message across.

'Mrs Rossi, I'm afraid I've got some bad news.'

Disquieting silence on the end of the phone. I could have done without this.

'Julia's in trouble.'

'Trouble, what kind of trouble?' she asked coolly.

Enrico, listening on the extension, started babbling.

'Enrico!' Something in Italian followed – 'Shut it!' I think she said.

'With the police.'

'Not money, I trust,' she asked. Though secretly I think she hoped it was. That was the one thing she could fix.

'No.' How did I explain this? 'Somebody's gone missing.'

'Oh, who?'

Girlfriend, partner, ex-lover?

'A friend,' I decided.

'So what has this to do with Julia, Letty?'

I took a deep breath. 'They think she's responsible.'

Silence from Sophia; sobs and curses from Enrico.

'When did this happen?' Sophia asked after she'd collected herself.

'Today, this morning, just now,' I babbled.

'Has she a lawyer?' she asked.

'Not as far as I know,' I admitted.

'Then take this number down.' Paper rustled for a

moment before she rattled off a local Manchester phone number. 'It's Mrs Orsini's private number. Tell her where Julia is and give her what details you know. Explain that you got her number from me. She is a lawyer of some renown. I would ring her myself, but I want to make immediate arrangements to fly to England. Could I possibly stay with you, Letty, at least until I can make other plans. Perhaps you can recommend a hotel near where Julia is held. We can discuss it tomorrow.'

I was too stunned by developments to interrupt.

'I will be travelling alone,' she stated abruptly. 'My husband will – how do you say it – hold the fort here. If I have any change of plans, I will let you know. Now, if you would excuse me, I must make some calls. Ciao, Letty.' And she was gone.

'And how did that go? As if I need to ask,' AnnaMaria enquired from the comfort of the armchair. 'There's more tea there for you,' she added.

I collapsed onto the settee and retrieved the much-needed mug from the floor. 'She's coming over.'

'When?' AnnaMaria asked suspiciously.

'Tomorrow.'

'She's not staying here, is she?'

I nodded and took a drink of tea. 'She'll be booking into a hotel as soon as she can.'

'Good,' AnnaMaria muttered. 'I'm stressed enough as it is. So what's next on the agenda?"

'I've got to ring this lawyer woman, a Mrs Orsini. She's a friend of Sophia's.'

'More likely a friend of her husband.'

'Don't jump to conclusions,' I ordered. 'You have a

terrible downer on Julia's family.'

AnnaMaria was silent for a moment, contemplating my comment, then, 'I wonder how Julia's coping?' she said. 'I don't suppose we can ring and find out, can we?"

'I doubt it,' I said. 'It's not as if she's in hospital. I'd better ring this solicitor and put her in the picture. At least I can do that.'

'Here,' AnnaMaria said. 'I'll do it. You go and have a bath or something. Put some clean clothes on. You'll feel a lot better.'

I breathed a sigh of relief and gave her the gist of what she had to say before leaving her to the phone. I went upstairs to get cleaned up. I wondered, as I doused myself, if the police had paid Sapphire a call and I made a mental note to contact her. But, as with most mental notes, I promptly forgot.

I wasn't gone long and when I got back AnnaMaria had sorted the lawyer out. 'She's ever so posh,' she said and laughed. 'If that accent can't help Julia, nothing can.'

We spent a quiet, frustrating afternoon, catching the local news on the television and the radio whenever we could. Newsflashes interrupted programmes all day. A missing MP could still send shock waves throughout the country. If she was controversial before, her untimely disappearance had suddenly put her up there with Lord Lucan.

Newswise there had been no further developments as far as we could tell, except unfortunately Julia's name had finally come to light.

I got a phone call from Milan at about four o'clock. It was Mrs Rossi letting me know she'd be in Calderton the following day. She was a very organised woman and she'd booked a hire car and made arrangements with the Ringway Hilton herself, so there would be no need for her to stay at the farm. I couldn't imagine her here somehow. But she would want to see me as soon as possible and would ring me on her arrival.

There was no arguing with her plans, so I just wished her a safe journey and, despite the circumstances, told her I was looking forward to seeing her again. I also told her not to worry and, optimist that I am, said we could sort this mess out.

Meanwhile I lived in dread of a call from the police or, even worse, my mother. It was just a question of time before she heard the news. Likewise Anne. And even if she wasn't news-watching, the women Anne was mixing with would surely hear on the grapevine.

What I didn't expect was another call from Janice.

Chapter 16

'My aunt sent me,' Janice explained, as I grudgingly let her over the doorstep.

Fortunately, AnnaMaria had gone for a lie-down. She was exhausted after the day's extraordinary events.

'Why?' I asked and motioned Janice into a seat. She was still clutching her camera and the notebook I'd seen her with earlier.

'To offer my help.'

'And what brought this on?' I was understandably curious. A couple of hours before she'd tried to buy my soul for a lift home.

She sighed, a sound much older than her years. 'My aunt blames me,' she began to explain. 'For what's happened. She said if it wasn't for me, Julia's good name wouldn't have been dragged into the papers.'

I had to suppress a smile. I didn't think Julia had a good name.

'I told her I only reported what I saw – it is my job, after all – but you know what she's like.'

Janice faltered. She'd had a pretty exciting day herself, one most journalists would gladly sacrifice a limb for. But we all lived in Calderton and rules tended to be different here. It wasn't normal practice for a neighbour to stab you in the back for a fee, not outside the village at any rate. Janice didn't need to explain further.

'So, how can you help?'

'Well, I can get you out of here for one thing,' she offered.

'Why would I want to get out?'

She checked her watch. 'Because in about ten minutes your farm is going to be overrun with reporters, cameramen, the BBC, ITV. Even *John Craven's Newsround* is going to be beating a path to your door.'

This was all delivered in such a deadpan manner, I couldn't help but despair at cynicism in one so young.

AnnaMaria, never one to miss much, appeared at the top of the stairs.

'You heard that?' I asked.

She nodded. 'Leave them to me.'

Disturbed from a half-sleep, she would eat Jeremy Paxman for breakfast.

'You get going. Ring me when you get a chance. If the cops call, I'll tell them I don't know where you are.'

Despite Julia's predicament, AnnaMaria was enjoying herself in some dark way. It was the anarchist in her. That child of hers was in for a very interesting life.

As a getaway car, Janice's B-reg Rover Metro left a lot to be desired, but it was anonymous and didn't warrant a second look from the passing newshounds as we hit the main road.

With AnnaMaria on the prowl, I felt I should give out

a public health warning. Though there was one thing about my lover's niece: she'd know what to say, and, more importantly, what not to say. Any skeletons would stay firmly in the closet.

'So where are we going?' I asked as Janice urged the decrepit vehicle along.

'Well, first I've got these for you.' She produced two pieces of paper from her inside pocket. 'From Julia.'

'How . . .'

She waved my question aside and instead indicated a right turn into the village itself.

'Read them,' she ordered.

Letty,
For God's sake get me out of here. Do you know what this place is like? It's disgusting, it's filthy and it stinks. And I've not done anything. They keep going over and over the same questions. They won't believe a word I say. I can't bear it, Letty. Please, try to get hold of my mother.

The second note was less hysterical, but no less demanding.

Letty, get me some fags – Gauloises, if you can – and give them to Janice. She can get them to me. Oh, and a comb, my Body Shop hair gel and some face wipes. This place is worse than a zoo.

Why wasn't I surprised at these requests?

Mrs Orsini's been to see me. Have you met her? She's gorgeous.

The woman was amoral.

They still keep asking me the same stupid questions. I don't know what's happened to Sita. I've not seen her for days. I keep telling them that.

The note blathered on.

My fingerprints are all over her car. They found it near Manchester Airport. Of course my prints are on it, we spent a lot of time in it, for God's sake. They found a gun too, at the garage.

I suppose a Daimler was one up from the back of an old Cortina. But that last piece of information was by far the most disturbing news I'd heard.

And they've got the note Sita sent me. The inspector said they could put it down as a crime of passion. We had the passion all right, but Christ, what's the crime? To listen to them you'd think they d already got the poor woman dead and buried, Letty. You've got to help me. I don't know what to do.

I could tell Julia was scared to death.

Mrs Orsini's told me not to say anything more to the police at the moment, but they won't let me out on bail. They keep saying I'm to be held pending further inquiries and I may have a court appearance tomorrow. My mother will go mad. Letty, you know I've had nothing to do with anything, don't you?

The note ended abruptly. Obviously written over a few hours, the letter showed that Julia's mood had taken a sharp downward swing.

The car suddenly came to a halt. We were outside Mrs Buckham's shop. To be honest, Mrs Buckham was the last person I wanted to see. Well, next to my mother. A curtain twitched in the parlour.

'Come on,' Janice ordered and she led me into the store.

The grocer's was closed for the afternoon.

'I've been mithered with reporters all day,' Mrs Buckham declared. 'I mean, what do I know?' she asked. What didn't she know more like. 'I wasn't even going to tell them where you lived. It was that stupid George,' she said crossly. 'Your next-door neighbour never could mind his own business. I had to throw him out of the shop in the end. He'll be in the pub now, knowing him, selling his story.'

She ground her teeth in irritation. Under other circumstances I would have liked nothing more than to gossip over such an event, but for obvious reasons now wasn't the time.

She bade me come and sit in the kitchen. It was a surprisingly cheerful place, unlike the shop itself, which, unchanged from the fifties (the 1850s) tended to look like a store in a Sam Peckinpah cowboy movie.

A small fire flickered in the kitchen hearth and a

chunky mug of tea and plate of parkin were forced into my reluctant hands.

'Now,' Mrs Buckham began, settling into a chair opposite, 'I've not brought you here out of nosiness. It just seems to me that us neighbours should stick together.'

Surreptitiously I glanced at the clock on the mantelpiece. The latest bulletin would be on soon.

'But Julia's a friend of mine too, you know.'

News to me.

'If she hadn't helped Janice get that nice car she drives around in, well, I don't know where I would have been. Since Bill died – ' her husband – 'I've had such problems getting to the cash and carry. I'm not as young as I was. But with Janice's job being part-time everything's worked out just fine. I've not got much family left now, you know.'

She sighed, reflecting on her losses over the years.

'Anyway, that's all by the by.'

I edged forward. To be honest, it was good to get out of the house. Problems seemed to loom larger there somehow.

'I hope you don't mind, but I had a wee look at that letter from Julia and, if you want my advice, I wouldn't show it to the police.'

'Well, it hadn't occurred to me to show them,' I said. 'Julia's solicitor has already told her to keep quiet. I wouldn't want to make things worse.'

'Very wise, very wise,' Mrs Buckham agreed. 'You know what they can be like. There's never been any police in my family. My husband would spin in his grave. Long memories, the Buckhams,' she added. 'More tea?'

She filled my cup with the strong brew and I forced a couple of mouthfuls of cake down my throat.

'I know we've not had our usual chat lately,' she said, seating herself once more. 'I realise you've been busy up at the farm, what with Anne leaving for America. Gosh, what a country that is. This sort of thing happens there all the time. Do you know, I can still remember what I was doing when Kennedy got shot. He was such a lovely man, so handsome. I never believed a word they said about him. I think it was the FBI, you know, that murdered him. Never trust a police agency named after a furniture store.'

She'd got me there.

'That's MFI, Auntie,' Janice corrected.

'Well, whatever,' she said and hitched her skirt further down her legs, annoyed at being interrupted.

She played with the teapot again, but I declined another drink – her toilet was up a flight of stairs so steep you'd have to be a mountain goat to negotiate it successfully.

'I don't blame AnnaMaria for hitting my Janice. You were more shocked than anything, weren't you, love?' she asked, turning to her patient niece. 'Anyway, it'll be her hormones. You'll have to get used to it in the next few months. It'll play havoc, you watch.' Though havoc with what she didn't explain. 'It's when the little one's born that the trouble really starts, isn't it?'

She went off into gales of laughter at that.

'I don't suppose there's any chance of a wedding, is there? We could do with things livening up a bit around here.'

'I think it's lively enough at the moment, Auntie,'

Janice commented drily.

'Mmm, maybe you're right,' Mrs Buckham agreed.

With one simple sentence, Janice had catapulted her aunt back to the problem in hand.

'That's why I wanted to see you really,' she confessed at last. 'Now, I'm sure you're getting all the help and advice you need from AnnaMaria and suchlike, and I understand that Julia's mum is coming over from Italy.'

I was too stunned to ask how she knew, only amazed that GCHQ hadn't snapped her up. With Mrs Buckham on the payroll the Cold War would have ended decades ago.

'But,' she said, lowering her voice (a case of 'the walls have ears'), 'I hear things in the shop, you know.' She tapped the side of her nose. 'People think you're deaf and blind just because there's a counter between you and them. But I'm not a doctor,' she said obscurely. 'I've not signed any oath. I can tell *who* I want, *what* I want.'

She folded her arms across her widening bosom and waited for a response.

'Oh, definitely,' I said, shaking and nodding my head at the same time. Surely one reaction was right.

Mrs Buckham beamed and squeezed my thigh with a firm and powerful hand. Despite her advancing years, she could still give a painful dead-leg should she wish.

Out of the corner of my eye I saw Janice check her watch. The biggest story in Britain was breaking on her doorstep and she was stuck at home waiting for her aunt to get to the point.

'So, if anybody should have this, you should,' she said and briskly got to her feet. 'Janice, what are you waiting for? Put the news on. Let's see what's happened to poor Julia.'

Janice didn't even bother sighing, just reached for the ageing black and white telly and switched it on. A couple of stages up from the cathode ray (where she got the valves from was anybody's guess), this Bakelite TV set was a collector's item. Any museum would have gladly had it in their 'Living History' exhibit, though Mrs Buckham would have had to come with the package.

It took a few moments to warm up and Mrs Buckham, obviously part Tibetan sheep, skipped upstairs to collect whatever it was she had for me.

Julia's face appeared on the screen. From a pinpoint, it filled the ten-inch frame in seconds. The police mug shot made Divine Brown look positively desirable by comparison.

Where were those full lips, that heavy-eyebrowed look, copied perfectly from Jack Nicholson's Jake in *Chinatown*? What had happened to the soft, floppy black hair, cut into a casually expensive style by Tristan at Vidal Sassoon? Whose was the dead cat on her head? And why had she got a black eye?

'Is that Julia?' Mrs Buckham asked, returning to the room.

The newsreader came on:

'Julia Rossi, a second-hand car dealer from Calderton, West Yorkshire . . .'

Julia would sue for that description!

'. . . is being held in custody at Bootle Street Police

Station in Manchester. The police are investigating the suspected abduction of Sita Joshi, MP for CalderVale. A spokesperson for Greater Manchester Police has just issued a statement.'

A Bobby Charlton haircut appeared and the screen went blank, probably in protest.

Mrs Buckham whacked the set with a well-practised hand. Welsh TV came on, the same programme in a different language. She switched it off.

'Janice, don't you think you ought to be at the *Echo*?' she asked.

Not needing much prompting, Janice was off like a shot.

'You still owe me an exclusive,' she reminded me before leaving.

'It's a funny business, all this,' Mrs Buckham observed.

A small package rested under one strong arm. Flat and oblong and wrapped in tissue paper, I couldn't guess what it was. She put it on the floor beside her. I knew better than to ask.

'First there's the bypass.' She looked at me closely. 'Now Anne's sister, that was an odd to-do. Not that I'm one to criticise her family.'

It seemed best not to add my thoughts.

'Oh, but that little one she looks after.' Mrs Buckham laughed with a memory she didn't want to share. 'She reminds me of Janice when she was just a tot. Looks a bit like her too.'

I couldn't see the resemblance myself. Janice was small and enthusiastic, a determined auburn-haired young woman. And Wallis was . . . Similar, I thought with a smile.

'So you've met them?' I asked.

'I should say!' Mrs Buckham sniffed. 'I've had the lot in here. Vegetarians, every one. No offence,' she added quickly, 'but I've had to freeze all my sausages. I got in extra, you know, when I heard we'd be having all these people camping. Tree protesters, they call themselves. Mmm, though there isn't much in the way of trees on Middleton Road, you know,' she said, echoing a comment I'd made myself. 'Anyway, there was no early-morning fry-up for them, though I managed to sell all the Alpen. Just as well. It was almost past the sell-by date.'

Mrs Buckham had obviously lost her train of thought. There was silence for a moment.

'A funny business,' she repeated quietly, retrieving the package. 'Now, I don't want you to get the wrong idea,' she began, carefully unwrapping the tissue paper. 'But I think you ought to see this before anybody else. Even Janice hasn't seen it. I'd have had to lock her in her room to stop her taking this to her editor, I can tell you. She's getting a bit old for that. And she's a bit too fast for me nowadays to be honest,' she added, smiling.

I found that hard to believe somehow.

To my surprise she produced a video. I don't know what I'd expected, but a video wasn't on the list of possibilities.

'Come upstairs,' she offered. 'I'll play it for you.'

Mrs Buckham's bedroom was the antithesis of her kitchen. It had more in common with Julia's abode than

137

a sixty-odd-year-old grocer's. I was privy to Mrs Buckham's little secret, however, and her wall-to-wall video collection of films old and new would have made Barry Norman reach for his film guide.

She had the back bedroom of the terraced house and, unusually for a structure built in Calderton shortly before the First World War, it had a bay window overlooking the whole of the area. With binoculars and on a clear day, it would be possible to see my farm.

Fastened to a wall at an angle above her state-of-the-art hydraulic bed, Mrs Buckham had a sixteen-inch, wide-screen colour TV and a Panasonic fourteen-day programmable video recorder. She also had an array of perfumes, make-up and face-care products on her Ikea dressing table that Zsa Zsa Gabor would have gladly endorsed.

'Sit on the bed,' she ordered. 'It's the best view.'

Pink, pink, pink was the colour of her room; even the carpet had a slight rose hue.

The TV came to life as I took in my surroundings. Julia was back centre stage, this time pictured on still photos taken outside her garage earlier that day. Somewhere in the background was me, thankfully too blurred to recognise.

My mother would surely have got wind of the news by now. Knowing my luck I'd have her and Julia's mother both at the farm together. I wondered if I should leave the country.

'. . . police are also hoping to question another woman to help with their inquiries. Letitia Campbell, also of Calderton . . .'

I'd obviously left it too late.

'. . . is a known associate of the woman held in custody.'

God if they questioned every known associate of Julia, the real criminal would die of old age. Mercifully the screen went blank. I decided to give the police a ring later. I couldn't face their questions yet.

The video began to roll.

Chapter 17

Now stunned is an underrated and overused word, but after viewing the short tape it was the only one that summed up my feelings.

'I didn't realise it would be important,' Mrs Buckham insisted as she rewound the tape. 'It was a miracle I kept it. I was short of a blank tape for *Gone With the Wind*, my old copy had snapped, and it was on Sky the other night. You didn't tape it by any chance? No? Never mind, it'll be on again. It's only the last hour that's missing.'

Mrs Buckham's eyes were suddenly far away, filled with the memory of crinoline dresses and debonair young men ready to scoop her in their arms at a moment's notice. A small pink tongue appeared to dampen her dry top lip in preparation for Rhett Butler's kiss.

I retrieved the tape from the machine as Mrs Buckham day-dreamed, eternally grateful it hadn't been chewed. Mum's BMW had made short shrift of the Kim Stove tape. The thought made me shudder, not for the tape's loss but that name. I'd hardly thought I'd hear much of it again, far less see her, her trips to England were so rare, but there she was, hazy but recognisable, caught on home video performing to an unexpected audience. The fact that she was in my village was almost too incredible to grasp.

'It's Janice's,' Mrs Buckham explained, producing a camcorder from the wardrobe. 'She was experimenting with it so she could use it when those protest people arrived. Now, I'm not very good with gadgets – ' she programmed her own video, that was good enough for me – 'but all you do,' she continued, fiddling with the lens, 'is point and press. As the actress said to the bishop.'

Her strange toot-toot of laughter accompanied the old joke.

She gave me a quick demonstration of her recently acquired skills. Cecil B de Mille she was not, though Tarantino would probably have appreciated the quirky angles.

'It was only by chance that I caught anything on the film. Janice had left the camera here and I couldn't resist having a go. It's got one of those infra-red thingies as well. It'll tape just as well at night as it does during the day. 'Course, I wasn't going to keep the tape, I do hate waste. It would be much more useful with a film on it. And then when I had a look and I saw all that money being passed about . . . Well, you never know what's going on nowadays, do you? It could have been drugs or anything.'

I realised Mrs Buckham wasn't going to shut up, at least not without some comment from me.

'Why didn't you show it to the police?'

'Letty! You know me better than that. What have the police ever done for us? Eh? Nothing, that's what. Where were they during the miners' strike? Cracking open a few heads, that's where.' She folded her arms. It was an angry gesture. 'Our Billy was never the same after that.'

Her cheeks flushed with the bitter memory of her brother, whose pit-working days had been prematurely brought to a halt.

We contemplated this unpleasant piece of history for a few moments.

'Still, I suppose I shouldn't dwell,' she said eventually, though this was hardly the first time we'd spoken about it. It wasn't surprising her feelings towards the police were less than charitable.

Mrs Buckham took a seat next to me on the bed and mopped her brow with a white cotton hanky, conveniently kept in the pocket of her pinny. Her clear skin glowed in the light of the bedside lamp.

'Do you remember the coloured fellow in America a couple of years ago?' she asked.

I raised an eyebrow at the sudden change in direction and her non-PC language, but didn't comment.

'Or is it black now? Anyway, ooh, what was his name? Not that OJ chap. Ooh, what *was* his name?' she repeated.

I could hear her brain clanking into top gear. Where were we going with this?

'Rodney!' she exclaimed. 'Rodney King! Terrible that was. See what I mean about the police? Shocking. Never got over that.'

I wasn't sure whether it was she who'd never got over it or Rodney.

It suddenly dawned on me what line of thinking Mrs Buckham was following. Memories of Thatcher's Britain and then her references to JFK, OJ Simpson and Rodney

King were too subtle for her own good. I half expected her to cry, 'The police done it!'

'I rang Mrs Choudry this morning. She works at the cash and carry.'

We were suddenly off on another tack altogether. I wanted to drag her back to the video, but she wouldn't be dragged.

'You wouldn't think she was a feminist to look at her.' Mrs Buckham was as full of surprises as a wasp's nest. 'She's been married for twenty years. She's got three lovely girls,' she added wistfully. 'Mr Choudry's all right. He doesn't say a lot – he probably doesn't get much chance in that household.' I got a brief toot of laughter again. 'But Amna, Mrs Choudry, reckons I'm right. She knows what prejudice is. They've all had it in for her.' She stopped abruptly.

'Who?' I prompted.

'Mrs Joshi,' she sighed sadly. 'They always try to shut people up. Malcolm X was another one.'

I had an idea where this political rant was coming from and what had prompted it. Mrs Buckham had a collection of what she loosely termed 'controversial tapes'. Based mostly on dead political figures (she felt her Marilyn Monroe biography should be included in this part of her collection), her compilation was still on the coffee table, clearly the last videos to have been viewed. Watching them for more than five minutes would wind anybody up. Julia always reckoned I was a conspiracy theorist; she'd obviously never listened to Mrs Buckham.

From somewhere in the depths of the shop a bell began to ring.

Mrs Buckham tutted. 'Can't they read?' she asked sternly. 'Isn't "Closed" clear enough?'

She got up to answer the persistent ringing.

'What about the video?' I asked.

My first thought had been to take it to the police anyway, but the shopkeeper's theories had a nasty way of insinuating themselves. Perhaps it would be better in the hands of Julia's solicitor, and I said as much to the old woman.

'They'd know what to do for the best,' she agreed. 'I suppose we've got to trust somebody.'

The bell rang again, more insistent than ever.

'I'd better answer that,' she said with a sigh and got to her feet. 'Come on, I'll show you out. Take care of that package mind, won't you,' she continued as I carefully made my way downstairs.

My instincts, faced with the almost sheer staircase, were to go down backwards, or maybe on my backside. They were more treacherous than MI5, though judging by Mrs Buckham's effortless descent she could have given Nureyev a run for his money.

A half-glass door separated the living quarters from the shop, and the front door, a solid wood affair, doubled as the main and the tradesman's entrance. My inability to negotiate the stairs gave me a bird's-eye view of what happened next and a two-second start.

'Now, I'll have a word with our Janice,' Mrs Buckham was saying as she reached the front door. 'Perhaps she can –'

She never got to finish the sentence. Turned sideways on, she barely got a glance at her attacker, just enough perhaps to raise an arm to deflect the full force of the baseball bat.

The sound of Mrs Buckham crashing to the floor with a shriek had me moving. Self-preservation guided my steps and the stairs were no longer an obstacle. I turned tail and fled, clearing the steps two at a time. The two balaclava-hooded figures were so close behind me I could almost feel their breath on the back of my neck.

The bedroom door was still ajar and I powered breathless and scared into the pink palace. I shut and bolted the door – thank God for bolts – almost directly into the face of the first figure. I could hear little cries coming from somewhere and it took me a moment to realise they were mine. A sudden violent vibration rocked the bedroom door. The baseball bat, useful for baseball, beating up old ladies and smashing through doors, was today being used for two of those three options. The door rocked again and a splinter drove itself sharply into my shoulder blade.

'What do you want?' I screamed, surprising even myself. 'The money's downstairs!'

I was answered by another thud. I pulled myself away from the door, the splinter agonisingly detaching itself from my flesh.

It's surprising what desperation will drive you to and how little thought is needed. An office chair was placed neatly by a pine desk. It had caught my eye because it, or something similar, would do for AnnaMaria's garage. It was also ideal for breaking a window.

The antique window was irreplaceable, but not as irreplaceable as my body, and I felt no regret as the upholstered piece of furniture disappeared through a mountain of leaded glass. A burglar alarm suddenly wah-wahed into life, and still the bedroom door continued to splinter. All I could do was follow the chair.

The fifteen-foot drop to the outhouse slightly to the left of the bedroom window looked, in the half-light of the early evening, like the Grand Canyon.

'A sprained ankle at most,' I muttered to myself. 'A broken neck,' another voice whispered in my head.

The bedroom door burst open and I caught a glimpse of a well-manicured and beringed hand reaching for my neck before I leapt.

I remembered the cold wind catching my face and then . . . nothing.

Chapter 18

I awoke ten seconds, ten minutes, ten hours later on a bed of shattered glass. It must have rained because my head was wet, and I raised a scratched hand to wipe my eyes. Red rain? I thought stupidly as blood dripped from my fingers. Tentatively I lifted my head to see what had happened to the rest of my body. After a scary moment I found that it was still in working order.

I sat up. No thoughts or memories to worry me, not even a 'I wonder why I'm here?' distraction. Dazed, I picked glass out of my throbbing hands. My shoulder was sore and my ankle ached.

Two noises and a dim recollection of recent happenings began to bring me back.

Wah-wah, wah-wah . . . I knew that sound, and a cry from somewhere nearby was familiar. A burglar alarm? Mrs Buckham crying for help? I got to my feet, though my head swam. Shakily I brushed myself down. My thick denim jeans had saved my legs from injury, yet my swelling ankle made me cry out. I leaned heavily against the outhouse wall as slowly my mind cleared.

I'd almost made it to the roof of the building when I'd jumped from Mrs Buckham's bedroom, but the tiles were damp and slippy with moss and I'd stumbled, falling heavily onto the shattered glass. Nothing was really clear after that. Memories of a baseball bat and, strangely, a manicured hand jostled for a place in my mind.

Mrs Buckham's cries suddenly stopped and breathlessly I tried my footing. My ankle wouldn't take my full weight, but with the outhouse wall for support I managed to limp-hop-limp to the side of the house.

Other sounds and other voices came at me through the dark. Any fight had gone out of me and my limbs were too tired, too painful, too heavy for flight.

So I threw up on my shoes. Undigested parkin and a cup of tea downed aeons ago unexpectedly made a reappearance. I could cope with that. It was the arrival of a suddenly remembered baseball-bat wielding maniac that bothered me.

I clung to the wall, silent and terrified, breathing through my mouth to stop myself screaming. It was only when AnnaMaria poked a pale face around the corner that I was able to react. And I promptly burst into tears.

For a seven and a half stone woman well into the early stages of pregnancy, she had no trouble hoisting me back to Mrs Buckham's house, hush-hushing me gently with every step.

The storewoman was a pale, frail shadow of her usual self. Crouched at the bottom of the stairs, Mrs Buckham was being comforted by Laura and Wallis.

'We've been looking for you,' AnnaMaria whispered. 'The police have been to the farm. I thought I'd better warn you. Laura gave me a lift down in the van.'

'Thank God for that,' I replied hoarsely. 'I thought everybody had gone deaf.'

The burglar alarm still continued its two-note bleat, feebler now, but still irritating.

'All the villagers are at the road protest. Laura was back at the farm.'

I glanced at Laura as AnnaMaria lowered me to the floor. The carpet felt wonderful after the bed of glass. I could see Laura was doing something more than just comforting the old woman, and Mrs Buckham, with an obviously broken arm (even to my untrained eye), was much calmer and less traumatised than she should have been. Shock, I supposed, until I heard the gentle chanting of Laura's sweet voice. Whatever Laura's healing skills were, somehow she'd sent Mrs Buckham into another galaxy. Her eyes were fixed on a far distant point and a small smile graced her mouth.

Laura paused and quietly asked if I was okay. I nodded, though I didn't really know for sure. I was one big ache and the temptation to sprawl across the floor almost overwhelmed me.

'The police and ambulance are on their way,' Anna-Maria murmured, not wanting to disturb Mrs Buckham's fragile peace. 'You can tell me what happened when they fix you up.'

Laura continued her chanting and the five of us presented a quiet calm instead of the usual hysterical mayhem when the emergency services arrived minutes later.

The spell was soon broken, though the feelings stayed with me for a long, long time.

Chapter 19

For the third time in as many days Calderton hit the news, though only the *Echo* carried it as the lead story. Janice again, even closer to the main event than before.

'Robbery,' Inspector Davenport had insisted to me (the same inspector who'd taken Julia in). 'With violence,' he'd added after a moment.

I'd had four stitches in my head, two in my shoulder and a tetanus shot in my backside, so don't talk to me about violence.

'I can't see any connection with Ms Joshi's disappearance,' he'd stated. 'We're looking for common criminals who have taken the opportunity for easy pickings when the village was empty.'

Rumour was that he'd already dragged half the road protesters in for questioning. Dreadlocks and noserings were obviously signs of a criminal mind. Sergeant Sam wouldn't be very pleased to have this interfering big-city cop shoving his nose into the road protest, which, peaceful so far, had been a local concern. 'Let him mind his business and I'll mind mine,' I could almost hear Sam chunner.

As the nurse had tugged painfully at my head, the inspector had bombarded me with questions about my incarcerated friend: When had I seen her last? About Sita: Had I ever met her? Did I have any idea where she could be?

I couldn't help him much, and Julia even less. The video that had promised so much had, not surprisingly, disappeared, along with Mrs Buckham's takings for the day. All her other stuff had felt the business end of a baseball bat. She'd be devastated. Some of her tapes were irreplaceable.

As far as Julia was concerned, I knew her twenty-four hours would be up soon – that point in proceedings when the police would have to charge her or organise a special magistrates' hearing to have the period of detention extended. Julia had said as much in her note. Anyway, I don't watch *The Bill* for nothing.

The inspector obviously watched it too and he pressed a card with his number on it into my hand. A big shaggy man in a Burtons suit, he took up most of the space around my hospital bed. His nose, as flat as my pillow, was a relic from pugilist days and his sinuses whistled along with his words.

'So you never met her?' he asked me once again about the missing MP.

I tentatively leaned back on my pillow and a pack of piranhas gnawed at my scalp. 'I don't follow the news much,' I attempted to explain. 'I didn't really know anything about her until she got together with Julia.'

His disbelief was as obvious as an atheist's promised

the Second Coming.

'They were lovers?'

'Yes.'

As if he didn't know, though, to give him his due, he managed to be neither critical nor smutty.

'Why didn't you come forward earlier?'

'I didn't know you were looking for me,' I lied.

'Still don't watch the news, eh?'

'I'm here now.'

Since when has not watching the news been an arrestable offence?

He asked me questions about the road protesters. He thought it strange they were mostly women – he probably thought it was some lesbian plot. I told him no more than I thought he should know, slim pickings at best, as events of a more personal nature had distracted me. Doubtless MI5 had infiltrated Laura's group. He could get his own information.

After ten minutes the nurse chased him out. Even she was sick of hearing him.

'She's got to rest,' she ordered. 'Come back tomorrow.'

With surprising fleetness of foot, he slipped out of the cubicle, but not before a last word through the curtains.

'You will be around, Ms Campbell, won't you? Feel free to use my number if you think of anything.' And with a last nasal whistle, he was gone.

The nurse followed him to check on Mrs Buckham, who was being prepped for surgery. Her arm needed pinning – the thought made my toes curl – and Laura was keeping her company. I felt her odd, otherworldly ways had been a major factor in getting Mrs Buckham to Halifax General with all her faculties intact. Without her, we would all have been screaming.

AnnaMaria trooped in with Wallis after my treatment and they gazed at me solemnly from the foot of the bed.

'What?' I asked loudly. The piranhas took another chunk.

Janice had arrived, upset and guilty, regretting returning to work when she had, though it was likely that the three of us would have ended up at the accident unit otherwise.

'You look awful,' Wallis chirped. 'Are you going to die?'

The child had a morbid sense of curiosity.

'Not yet, I hope.'

'You've got to stay in overnight,' AnnaMaria explained. 'For observation.'

The nurse had already informed me and I was preparing myself for the dangers of hospital food. The X-rays, taken earlier, had been clear, though it wasn't recommended that you run around after a bang on the head. And with the extras from a Jacques Cousteau documentary burrowing into my skull, I wasn't about to argue.

The nurse bustled in again. 'Time for sleep,' she said and popped the skin on my arm with a sharp needle. 'Out, out, out,' I heard her say before a great grey blanket settled peacefully over my head.

After giving me the best eight hours' sleep of my entire life, I would gladly have given the nurse a medal. Sadly, my guarantees of a further good night's kip were short-lived and by nine the next morning I was being shipped out.

AnnaMaria, as reliable as ever, had brought Wallis and fresh clothes.

'The chickens are fine. Mrs Buckham will be fine. Plenty of R&R should fix her. Julia's still locked up, so she's okay, though there's no sign of Sita yet. However . . .' She paused for effect.

I struggled with a shoe. My ankle, sprained but otherwise undamaged, wouldn't co-operate and my laces were stretched to ridiculous lengths.

'However?' I urged as I tentatively tried my ankle. Anything less than agony and I could cope.

'Julia's mother's arrived early. She's at the cop shop as we speak.'

'She's scary,' Wallis insisted.

There was no answer to that. This from a girl who thought my mother was great. There's no accounting for taste.

'And your mum's been on the phone, but don't panic, she's in Brussels.'

'Brussels! What the hell's she doing there?"

'It's a business trip with her boss. I persuaded her you were okay, but she says to ring her as soon as poss.'

No problem putting that off.

'Anything from Anne?' I asked hopefully. If ever I needed some TLC from my loved one, now was the time.

'No phone calls,' AnnaMaria said gently. 'But don't worry. I'm sure she'll be in touch soon.'

The fax had been suspiciously quiet. Already I'd had her dead and buried, another victim of Los Angeles gangs (I wasn't married to the news, but not everything passed me by); romping in bed with k d; learning a mean forehand from Navratilova; and consorting with Hillary Clinton, who, I knew, she had a crush on. It didn't occur to me that the news wouldn't have reached her yet,

Calderton hardly being the centre of the universe.

So, after a quick visit to Janice and Mrs Buckham (who would probably sleep the day away), and armed with a bag of ripped and filthy clothes, I hobbled out of the hospital with Wallis, as untouched by events as only a five-year-old (nearly six, she'd insisted) can be, skipping along by my side and AnnaMaria gently holding my hand. As my lover's niece enthusiastically described the newspaper coverage of Sita's disappearance (and to be honest she took some delight in recounting Julia's involvement), it was sheer chance that I caught sight of a black Mini, its engine purring angrily, parked at an odd angle in an ambulance space. It took off at speed and hurtled past us, the backdraught plastering my jacket against my body.

'Fucking nutter,' AnnaMaria muttered.

A hand rested nonchalantly through the window of the passenger door. Long-fingered and elegantly ringed, it was a hand I would never forget.

Chapter 20

It took AnnaMaria a moment to calm me down and, as tempted as she was to give chase, the vehicle would be long gone by the time we could get to Laura's van.

'I got the number,' Wallis chirped as we reached Laura and her van.

'What number?' AnnaMaria asked as we clambered into the vehicle.

'From that fast car,' she said proudly.

'She's got a thing about car number plates,' Laura revealed, as she helped us in. She'd seen the brief incident but didn't realise its significance until I explained.

'My God,' she said. 'Wallis, honey, tell me the number.' She started the van. 'Perhaps you ought to tell the police,' she added somewhat grudgingly. Her experiences with the forces of law and order hadn't always been good.

'I dunno,' I said, recovering from the shock.

Mrs Buckham's words about not trusting anyone still

reverberated in my mind. Perhaps the bang on my head was making me paranoid. Though there was one person who could find out. It would probably cost me, but Janice could trace the owner of the Mini. Her aunt had already told me the sorts of tricks of the trade she indulged in – things that weren't quite legal but the police turned a blind eye to. Reverse phone books were one, where you could find an address if you knew the number, and tracing car registration plates was another if you knew whom to ask. It was worth a try anyway and was probably much safer than giving chase.

It was only later that I realised I could have saved Janice the trouble if my memory had been that bit better.

AnnaMaria took the well-remembered number from Wallis, who delivered it in a singsong voice reminiscent of times-tables learned by rote as a child. I carefully tucked the piece of paper into the back pocket of my jeans.

Exhausted already, I declined Laura's offer of a police visit and suggested we go home.

'How's the protest coming along?' AnnaMaria asked her, giving me space away from my immediate problems.

Laura smiled. 'We've set up camp now and the police haven't been too bad yet. The landowners haven't even sent in private security, which is a miracle. That's usually what happens next.' She paused to light a cigarette. 'There's been rumours, though. Have you heard anything?'

'Like what?' AnnaMaria asked.

I looked up from the *Daily Mirror* I'd found on the van floor. Sita Joshi's handsome face was plastered all over it.

'That the procedures for the bypass haven't been entirely legal.'

'First I've heard, though I've had other things on my mind to be honest,' I said, distracted by my aching head.

'It's possible there's some big council scam going on – you know, backhanders, that sort of thing. And a cock-up where legalities haven't been observed. Each person affected, whether a business owner like you, AnnaMaria, or just someone who rents a room in a house, should have proper legal sighting and notification of the proposed plans.'

'Well, we've not had that,' AnnaMaria said.

'Exactly. And that article in the paper? Where did that come from, eh? I'd have another word with that reporter if I were you. So it's all on hold. At least for the time being,' she added.

'I suppose that's something,' I muttered, though at this moment in time I didn't care if they built Manchester's third airport on it, with Concorde landing twice a day.

Breaking old habits, I went back to the paper.

Erik squawked his approval when I arrived home. Thundering up and down his coop, his beak drumming against the wire mesh, the twanging metal echoed a chorus of, 'Feed me, feed me now!'

AnnaMaria, having lived at the farm long enough, recognised the restless signs.

'If that chicken eats much more,' she said, 'he'll explode.'

Wallis, holding my hand, paused for a moment to consider this statement.

'You'll have to put him on a diet,' she said firmly. 'My mum was on a diet. She was frightened of getting stuck down a hole.'

For obscurity value, Wallis' comment took the biscuit. I looked to see if AnnaMaria could offer an explanation.

'Don't ask me. Kids, what are they like?'

Wallis danced over to the coop and had a chat in chicken language with Erik.

'Aunty Letty,' she shouted to me from across the drive. My heart warmed at the endearment. 'Can I feed Erik and see if there are any eggs?'

'If you find one you can have it for tea, with chips if you want.'

Her eyes lit up. Chips were a treat usually denied her and, with Laura still in the van and out of earshot, it could be our little secret.

Wallis opened the gate and Erik, not one to hang about, belted out of the run and made for my newly sprouting lawn. His various girlfriends and offspring sauntered after him, wings a-flapping in the chill spring sunshine.

It was a moment of normality in an otherwise chaotic world.

'Look, I'm going to have to get going,' Laura informed me from the van. 'Is it okay if Wallis stays with you? I may be gone a while.'

'I'll keep an eye on her,' AnnaMaria offered. Perhaps she was getting some practice in.

I hobbled towards the front door.

'Hang on a minute,' Laura shouted.

I turned as she climbed from the van.

'Letty, I've got something for you.'

She tucked a strong arm under mine and helped me into the house. AnnaMaria followed Wallis on her hunt for chicken feed and eggs.

The house wasn't as I'd left it. It was clean, tidy and spotless. Not Mum's work – everything would have been rearranged. Surely not AnnaMaria's – cleaning up was anathema to her, though her work on the attic had been surprising.

'Did you do this?' I asked Laura.

She smiled. 'Me and Wallis had a hand in it,' she admitted. 'The flowers are from AnnaMaria, though.'

The pine table, fitted out with an ironed tablecloth, was adorned with a multitude of spring flowers. A card was propped against it, as was a fax.

'Read the fax,' she suggested, helping me into a chair.

Suddenly her sister was reflected in her gentle ways and I felt a closeness towards Laura that hadn't really been there before.

'I'll make tea,' she said.

The fax was from Anne, of course, clearly ignorant of Calderton's troubles.

It was a love letter, the kind that ages, tied in ribbon, in a box beneath your bed. Its PS was full of facts, though. She was in Washington preparing for departure, and Carolina was the next stop. A new fax number was in one corner.

Have you written? I've not heard anything, but I'm on the move all the time. It's fantastic and the tours are going so well. I was nervous at first but I'm getting used to it now. Ring the new number QUICKLY before

I leave Washington. I love you, Letty.
I miss you, the farm, Calderton, even Erik.
Write me,
Your true love,
Anne XXX

PPS One of the women has just told me about the missing MP. An Asian woman, she said. An out dyke too. My God, what next!?
Let me know the gossip.

Kisses, darling XXX.

It would be easier to send the morning papers than try and explain. Even the *Mirror* had managed a decent factual explanation of what had happened, avoiding the lurid lesbian storyline that I knew some papers wouldn't be able to resist. But at least Anne's fax had set my mind at ease. She was obviously alive and kicking, or at least alive and talking. She wasn't bedding k d or examining Martina's portfolio, and Hillary Clinton's bedside manner was still a mystery to her.

'Good news?' Laura asked, handing me a cup. She took a seat opposite me.

'Well, she's not coming home yet, but things are going well.'

Understandably, I was reluctant to share my intimate feelings.

'Has she heard the news?' Laura asked carefully. She blew on her tea to cool it, gaze fixed firmly on the liquid.

'Some,' I said, 'but not the details. I'll try and get hold of her later. Do you want to send her a message?'

'No, no,' Laura said hurriedly. 'It'll keep.'

'Whatever,' I said, surprised at Laura's reluctance. Not my problem, I decided.

'Give me your foot,' she demanded after a moment. 'Let's see if I can't make it feel a bit better.'

Obliging, I heaved my leg onto her knee and removed my shoe. Alternating waves of pain and relief flooded my battered foot. The cup she'd been blowing, which I discovered didn't contain tea at all, was retrieved from the table. It held a thick, odourless fluid, brown in colour, which she stirred carefully with a spoon.

'Trust me, okay?' she said.

She began to chant and my British reserve, handed down through generations, blocked her for a moment. Embarrassed and tense, I started to withdraw my leg. She held it with one firm hand. As arm-wrestlers, Laura and Mrs Buckham would have been unbeatable.

'Breathe deeply,' she commanded. 'Trust me,' she repeated.

Remembering long-ago night-school yoga lessons, I took her advice and soon her words, sung too low to understand, began to affect me.

Tea was forgotten, even the pain in my stitched head was forgotten, and I lost myself, despite myself, to a rite centuries old.

A sudden warmth engulfed my ankle, the liquid somehow turning instantly to ice as it was daubed generously on my foot. The last vestiges of pain left me and, after a few minutes, I could feel, rather than see, the swelling subside. My foot felt like mine again.

Laura's chanting faded. She wrapped my ankle in a type of gauze that I'd never seen before. 'Leave it on for a week and, if I'm able, I'll do this again,' she murmured mysteriously. 'Put your shoe on. See if your foot will take your weight.'

It was fine, of course, though not completely strong yet. I couldn't run a marathon, but then again I'd never wanted to.

Chapter 21

'So tell me about the video, then,' AnnaMaria demanded as she handed me a cup of coffee.

I'd escaped to my bedroom for a lie-down after Laura left to go and check on Gran. I'd only met the older woman once. A strange and insular character, she clearly loved her granddaughter but didn't have much to say to the rest of the world.

About my mother's age, they were as far removed from each other as it was possible for two people to get. Well turned out, expensively coiffured and aerobics fit, Margaret Campbell was new *Cosmo* woman, or at least her elegant mother. Wallis' gran had more in common with Earth Mother, a cross between Germaine Greer without the gob and Anita Roddick without the credit cards. Her fair hair showed not a trace of grey and her skin, unlined apart from tiny crow's feet around her eyes, was as unblemished as a twelve-year-old's. Her physique had been developed by exercise of a more hands-on type. I couldn't imagine her in a gym somehow. If Wallis stayed on the road, she could expect to look like her gran in fifty years' time.

'She used to teach,' Laura had said, revealing Gran's past as we'd shared a brew after her ministrations. 'She's Aussie by birth, like Wallis, as I'm sure she's told you.' Laura smiled, remembering. 'She taught PE at a girls' school for a while. She moved to the bush. She hated the city and she wanted a healthier life for Juliette, her daughter – Wallis' mum,' she'd added quietly. It was funny, that was the first time she'd used her dead lover's name.

'It was through her that I met Juliette. We took climbing lessons together.'

Laura paused once more and for the second time I saw her grapple with a thought that she was tempted to share. Again she resisted. I almost pressed her, but something in her expression stopped me, that and my own growing exhaustion. I'd had enough tragedies of my own for the time being.

The sudden arrival of the press had stopped any further conversation and I'd withdrawn to my bed. Laura had escaped through the back door, leaving AnnaMaria to deal with the unwelcome visitors. Not surprisingly, they didn't hang around for long.

I managed to doze for a couple of hours before curiosity and the growing news coverage drove AnnaMaria upstairs with a coffee. As the only available person within three thousand miles I trusted, I'd divulged the news to AnnaMaria earlier of the existence, if only briefly, of Mrs Buckham's video tape. Hours later, propped up in bed, I watched her jaw drop as I gave her a quick verbal replay.

'Kim Stove?' she muttered quietly. 'I don't understand.'

'No,' I agreed. 'Neither do I.'

'So the attack on you and Mrs Buckham was just for the tape?'

'I think so,' I said. 'Though they took the day's takings.'

'And whoever you saw in the Mini at the hospital was the same person?'

I nodded.

'Oh, Christ,' I said, suddenly reminded. 'I forgot to ring Janice about the number plate.'

My memory was going. Perhaps the blow on the head was more serious than the hospital thought.

'I'll do it,' AnnaMaria offered, rooting in my jeans for the piece of paper.

'And while I think on,' she said, 'there's another fax for you.'

I hobbled only slightly on my much-improved ankle and, while a rat up a drainpipe might have been quicker, it was unlikely to have been as enthusiastic. My earlier efforts to contact Anne had met with failure. First the new number had been engaged and later it wouldn't pick up.

Disappointingly, this new communication was from my mum, though I shouldn't really complain. She was worried about me, bless her, and a quick letter to her mobile fax would put her mind at ease.

I tried Anne again and this time my letter (long and complicated) was devoured by the machine. Whether it would reach her before she hit Carolina was another matter. To be honest, she was better off out of it.

I had a quick wash to liven myself up while AnnaMaria rang Janice. Dousing myself in water, I had five minutes to reflect on these roller-coaster events. I didn't dwell on them too long, for that way madness lay.

'Janice will be in touch when and if she can find out. She's itching for a story.'

'I can imagine,' I murmured. 'If all this sorts itself out, she'll be the first to know.' '

'What happens now, then?' AnnaMaria asked.

She was obviously rocked by what I'd told her about the video. Her heroine had been caught doing dodgy dealings on tape and she, like me, couldn't figure out why.

'Do we involve the police again?'

'I dunno,' I mused as I watched Wallis, lost in concentration, draw a credible picture of Erik on a sketchpad. She was crouched on a high stool at the kitchen table and I was envious of her innocence.

The phone rang as I gently towelled my hair dry and the voice at the other end galvanised me into action.

'Letty?' Julia shrieked. 'I'm out.'

'God, where are you?' I shrieked back.

AnnaMaria looked alarmed. Wallis continued drawing.

'With my mother, at the Hilton. You know, near the airport.'

Oh, yes, silly me. I was a frequent visitor.

'Can you come over?' she begged. 'I'll buy you dinner,' she bribed unnecessarily.

'Of course,' I said. 'Though I'm bringing AnnaMaria and Wallis.'

'Fine, fine,' she replied. 'Whatever.'

Fine? She must have misheard.

'We'll be over at about – ' I checked my watch – 'six. How's your mum?'

She paused.

'Coping,' Julia sighed. 'Can you get me some clothes from the flat on the way? I don't want to go in case there are reporters. Get the blue skirt suit, the Galliano one. You know what Mum's like about me and trousers. And a couple of white shirts. Oh, and clean underwear. I don't want to have to wear these knickers another day. Mrs Orsini, remember, my solicitor? She told me about the attack on the shop. Are you okay? Is Mrs Buckham all right? Is it something to do with Sita, do you think?' She was babbling on nonstop.

'Yes, yes and yes,' I replied. 'I'll tell you more when I see you. Galliano suit, white shirts and underwear, right?'

'Right, and some tights,' she added. 'I'll see you in a bit.'

I replaced the phone in its cradle and turned to AnnaMaria.

'Fancy dinner at the Hilton?' I asked.

Julia was right about the reporters. By some miracle they'd missed her sudden departure from the cells (more strings pulled by the high-flying Mrs Orsini?), but they'd set up camp outside her flat. They'd arrived en masse, a ream of reporters standing around in the deepening gloom. It was obvious they believed their own hype about the inner city. No front-line Bosnia reporting for this shower. To my relief, there was no sign of Janice.

I ran the gauntlet (or hobbled) to Julia's flat and was ignored, thanks to my new disguise. Carrying an old set of clothes under a new dry-cleaning bag, I was simply running an errand. I knew that one day all the lesbian PI novels I'd ever read would come in useful. I had to bang on the door to gain entrance and the doorman, who recognised me, either didn't give a toss or was happy with the tenner I gave him. Either way, I made it upstairs to Julia's flat unhindered. Only the blue and white crime-scene tape across Julia's door stopped me in my tracks. I had no idea whether it was legal for me to cross it or not. What lay behind the door? Did I want to find out? Feeling that I didn't have much choice, I fumbled with the lock.

I'd expected the flat to be a shambles after the police search, but it was only slightly disturbed. I didn't hang about and grabbed the required clothes. Old money-bags Julia owed me for this.

Despite the loan car of Julia's (I hadn't got round to returning it), the trip to the airport was uneventful, though the police presence could be felt. The force's search teams were still out and about. I could imagine the relief the residents of Hulme and Moss Side would be feeling as the police helicopter buzzed over a different area for a change. The news of Sita's disappearance had been relegated to second billing on Radio Four, though news of Julia's release had been leaked at last.

An underpaid lackey parked the car for us on our arrival at the hotel. His sniff of disapproval could be heard at Terminal 2. He was more used to Bentleys and Rollers than this second-hand (probably fifth-hand) Volkswagen of Julia's.

However, the staff on duty indoors had, I think, made an assumption about our small group as soon as we stepped over the threshold. Eccentric and rich, we'd dressed down for the occasion. I tried not to say too much – my accent was a dead giveaway, though I wasn't sure whom I was trying to impress.

We waited in the wilderness that was the reception area as the well-off bustled around us. The place smelled of money. A couple of Chanels walked past and the odd Dior wafted by. I had to stop Wallis from holding her nose. We'd both spent too long with chickens to appreciate the finer things of life.

Finally Julia's mother made an appearance. Her dress, of fine blue wool, clung to that marvellous figure – she would have looked gorgeous wrapped in tin foil. She held out her hands in greeting and kissed me European style, on both cheeks, tutting sympathetically over my recently acquired injuries.

She welcomed AnnaMaria warmly. Wallis was apprehensive when Mrs Rossi's attention was focused on her. At five, I would have found the woman scary too.

We ploughed our way through the lush Hilton carpet to a smooth and silent lift. Mrs Rossi, comfortable with children, animals and royalty, made a play for Wallis' affections and by the time we hit the eighth floor the little girl had presented Julia's mum with the picture of Erik. Fickle, Wallis abandoned both me and AnnaMaria and clutched instead at Mrs Rossi's hand.

Wading through more acres of carpet, we finally arrived at room 801. Julia gazed gloomily through the half-opened door. She looked terrible. In just a couple of days she'd lost pounds, her face was drawn and white, and the black eye she'd somehow acquired was fading to a sickening green and yellow.

'God, you look like shit,' she muttered to me before I had a chance to utter a greeting.

'Looked in a mirror lately?' AnnaMaria sniped back.

Julia ignored the remark and ordered me into the

bedroom with her while she got changed. Mrs Rossi took charge of the rest of the party.

Julia's Hilton bedroom would have happily engulfed the whole ground floor of my farm. A queen-size bed, complete, for some reason, with a silk mosquito net, took up the central space. Built-in maple wardrobes covered an entire wall. Even Liz Taylor would have been well catered for.

'So they let you out, then?' I asked as I lowered myself onto the bed's plush cover.

'Finally,' she snapped, stripping off with obvious relief. This was far and away the grubbiest I had ever seen Julia. Her underwear looked as if someone had used it to clean the cell floor.

'They've got nothing on me,' she yelled, disappearing into the en-suite bathroom.

'Do you think I don't know that?' I replied, staring at the ornate ceiling. The rose around the light fitting, obviously stolen from a stately home, was edged in gold and, as a fashion accessory, was completely at odds with the exterior of the modern hotel complex. The cornice was painted to match and the walls, opulent in mulberry, were inspired by an interior designer who dreamed of decorating the set for *Carry on Cleo*.

'How much has this little lot cost?' I asked idly, stretching luxuriously on the down quilt.

'Don't ask me. That's Mum's department,' Julia replied, wandering past wrapped in the whitest and fluffiest of towels. 'Look at the state of me,' she exclaimed, lowering herself onto a pink chintzy stool that Mrs Buckham would die for. She gazed miserably at her reflection in the dressing-table mirror. 'I don't believe this,' she moaned. 'And Sita! Where the hell is she?'

I didn't like to remind her that the press had already buried her. The blood on the car seat, the gun found in Julia's garage and absolutely no sign of the woman pointed to only one thing.

'It's all a load of old crap, you know,' Julia stated firmly. 'That blood they found in the Daimler? Chicken's blood! Not even human. I'd check your stock if I were you,' she muttered darkly.

I sat up in surprise. 'Who told you that?'

Julia began rubbing her bruised skin with face cream. 'Do you know how I got this?' she demanded, ignoring my question.

'Resisting arrest?' I offered.

'That's what *they* say,' she said, but wouldn't offer an alternative explanation. 'And that gun they found? Never been fired, much less by me. Stupid bastards,' she added in Italian, the only two words she'd chosen to teach me. 'I think she's been kidnapped. I'd know if she was dead.'

There was no questioning the absolute certainty of Julia's statement.

'And do you know why they let me out?'

A reply would have been surplus to requirements.

'Inspector Davenport has got it into his head that I'll lead them to her.'

'And he's said that, has he?' I asked.

'Well, no, he won't, will he? But it's obvious, isn't it?' she snapped.

Julia had leapt from misery to fury in the space of five minutes. It's surprising what a pair of clean knickers will do.

'So what's your story, then?' she asked, struggling into

navy opaque tights. The skirt followed. She really did have a great pair of legs.

I rushed verbally through my ordeal.

'And the police think there's no connection!' Julia snorted. 'And that video, what was on it exactly?'

Her reaction when I told her was the same as AnnaMaria's.

'But I thought Kim was on tour.'

'So did I,' I said, recalling the details of the tape.

'And it was definitely money being exchanged?'

'Oh, yes.' I confirmed. 'I saw it being counted.'

The short film had caught two figures. Kim Stove's face had been clearly outlined by streetlights. The other, the one that had counted the cash, was huddled in the front seat of a car. It had been impossible to distinguish any features.

The tape had left me with more questions than answers, questions that Julia bombarded me with.

'Why the hell was she in Calderton? What was the money exchanged for? You said yourself it seemed a lot, and who,' Julia asked, using her fingers to emphasise the point she wanted to make, 'was the other person?'

'Quite,' I said, unable to shed any light.

'Letty, why didn't you tell the police? I wasn't that keen on languishing in the cells, you know.' She grinned at me lopsidedly, tempering the words.

I paused and stared at the ceiling once more before I answered. 'I don't know' wouldn't do.

I didn't think they'd take me seriously,' I managed after a moment. 'It might have meant nothing.'

'Yeah, right.' Julia sighed.

'For one thing, Mrs Buckham was out of it by then.

She was hardly in a position to back me up. The tape was gone. And . . .' I faltered.

'And?'

'What Mrs Buckham said, about not trusting the police. You know the trouble her family's had with them in the past. It stuck with me.'

Julia tutted and went back to her ablutions. 'Never mind her family. That woman watches too much TV,' she said.

There was a sudden rap on the bedroom door.

'Julia,' Mrs Rossi called, 'dinner has arrived. Please hurry. I'd hate it to spoil.'

Julia donned her white shirt and jacket. Her hair, clean and glossy, held no comparison to the limp mess shown on her mug shot. Despite the skirt, she looked like the Julia I knew and loved.

Mrs Rossi did what all good mothers do when their chick is in trouble, she provided a decent feed and a little fuss. Dinner, as I'd suspected, was a banquet fit for the Three Tenors. We were taken through servings of Italian food that I'd never seen before. Not even in Marks. It was a far cry from the ciabatta and antipasta that I reckoned to be classy food. Only the crisp salad and tomatoes, drizzled with the finest extra virgin olive oil, were remotely familiar. The final offering was a delicate, if un-traditional, tiramisù.

Wallis had egg and chips.

Whereas technology had sealed the little girl's friendship with my mother, a more basic bond had been made with Sophia Rossi.

*

Wallis dozed after a while and her new friend retired to her bedroom to make international connections with her fretting husband. AnnaMaria was glued to the TV, making sure we were kept abreast of any developments. Julia and I cracked open a bottle of wine, but before we could lose our senses to it Julia's phone beeped into life. Reluctantly she put her glass on the coffee table and keyed the pad.

'Hello,' she said.

There was a slight and telling pause before her face drained of colour.

Chapter 22

'Sita?' Julia asked in a choked voice.

AnnaMaria hurriedly joined us on the settee. Three pairs of ears strained around Julia's mobile phone.

'Sita, honey, where are you?'

A faint cultured voice echoed over the tinny airwaves. 'I really don't know,' she said and laughed nervously.

'Are you all right?' Julia squeaked. Her voice threatened to desert her completely.

'Fine, yes. I'm fine,' she said. Sudden tears proved otherwise.

'Julia, please.'

A mumbled exchange in the background and the phone went dead.

'One, four, seven, one,' AnnaMaria muttered. 'Do one, four, seven, one.'

I took the phone from Julia's nerveless fingers and stamped out the numbers breathlessly, hoping to reveal the whereabouts of the last caller.

The voice of BT, never one to be rushed, obligingly

divulged the numbers. I muttered them over and over again as AnnaMaria tore the place apart looking for a pen. Just like lottery night, there was never one to hand when you were convinced that you'd won.

Finally, the numbers safely on paper, I looked at a silent Julia, so pale she seemed green. She was almost the same colour as her shiner.

'Julia, Julia, snap out of it,' I ordered.

AnnaMaria took it upon herself to inflict violence and she pinched my old friend viciously above the elbow.

'Ow!' Julia said as her eyes refocused. 'There was no need for that.'

'Now what?' I asked. My voice had gone up an octave. 'Are you going to ring her back, call the police, what?' I thought for a moment as Julia downed her glass of wine in one. 'It was definitely Sita, wasn't it?'

'Of course it was,' Julia said. 'Let me look at that number again. I knew she wasn't dead, I just knew it.'

'Yeah, but we still don't know where she is, do we?' AnnaMaria stated. 'She didn't sound as though she was having a bundle of fun, did she?'

Making a sudden decision for all of us, AnnaMaria took the phone from Julia and dialled.

'Switched off,' she said after a moment. 'Don't you think we should call the police?'

'No way,' Julia stormed, loud enough to disturb a sleepy Wallis. 'Do you know how hard it was to get out of their clutches? Do you have any idea how I suffered? My God, if you think I'm going to just fling myself back into their arms again, well, you can think again. And that cell!' she stormed. 'Letty! Your chickens have better quarters.'

To listen to Julia, you'd think she'd been incarcerated with Terry Waite.

'Julia,' Mrs Rossi interrupted, returning to the lounge, 'is there a problem?'

I nudged AnnaMaria before she could blast Sophia with a flippant reply. A quick conversation in Italian followed between mother and daughter and then a look of concern clouded Mrs Rossi's brow.

'If my husband was here,' she said to me with a shrug, 'we could find Julia's friend, even with so little information, but England is not my home. I do not know how these problems are resolved here.'

Her veiled hints, from anybody else, would have been chilling, but Mrs Rossi, who had seen absolute poverty as a child, was a pragmatist. Her beloved daughter needed protecting, therefore she would protect. It was as simple as that. But despite this backbone of steel (and a demeanour of silk), Mrs Rossi had nowhere to turn.

She may not have been in a position to help, but I knew someone who was.

Chapter 23

Janice had become Calderton's very own star. With access denied to reporters of a more substantial calibre, the local newshound had grabbed this rare opportunity with both hands.

The photos she'd snapped after Julia's arrest and subsequent release (she had been the only one to get wind of that information, leaked by a regretful and increasingly hormonal AnnaMaria) had been taken up by the big dailies. One or two had made it to the *Evening Post*, delivered with dinner by a fully liveried bellboy.

Janice's mobile number had been given to me by Mrs Buckham in an odd moment of foresight. 'In case you ever need her, dear,' she'd said, patting my knee. 'Not for my sake,' she'd added hurriedly. 'Don't worry about me. I sometimes think I'll outlive the lot of you. No, one day you may just need her help.'

Obediently I'd entered the number in my sometimes barren diary. At least it had been so until my girlfriend's fame and fortune had begun to spread. There were several 'J' entries now. Jessie from Canada was one. A woman priest in a gay subdivision of a radical Baptist ministry, we'd had a flying visit from her one weekend. She'd wanted Anne's autograph on her copy of *Babylon, Then and Now* and I hung around long enough for her to realise that was all she was going to get. I don't know whether all Baptist ministers are as randy as Jessie, but this particular priest's morals had been hatched somewhere in the sixties. As far as stories were concerned, Janice could have done worse than interview the Canadian. She was easily on a par with any wayward Catholic priest.

But before I could make the call I was tempted by another option. Inspector Davenport's card fell from my diary, white and embossed, showing not only his office number but his mobile too. I was suddenly faced with an agonising choice. It would have been no contest to most people, to let the police deal with it would have been easy. But I had Julia in my ear (she changed her mind as often as her outfits), and a severe case of stupidity, which I blamed on my bang on the head.

Stupidity won and I rang Janice from the surreal and luxurious splendour of the Hilton. Buried in a settee the size of a grand piano, I caught Mrs Buckham's niece loitering outside the hotel.

'Janice,' I said despairingly, realising she must have followed us, 'you could have come up, you know.'

The night had quite settled in and a cold yellow moon shone equally over the righteous and the damned. The strange gloom suited Janice's melancholic mood and reluctantly she agreed to exchange the dubious comforts of her Metro for the grandeur of Room 801.

I couldn't see the dilemma myself.

Janice had aged five years in as many days. Clutching the ubiquitous Nikon, her bleary eyes were first into the room.

'Goodness,' Mrs Rossi said, surprise overcoming politeness. 'Let me order some coffee.'

'Thanks,' Janice said and collapsed into the vacant settee. The rose-pink upholstery threatened to swallow her frail form.

'How's Mrs Buckham?' AnnaMaria asked, keeping a comfortable distance between them.

'She's still a bit ropy,' Janice declared, 'but she'll be fine.'

She began to search through her many-pocketed coat. Though dyed black, its army origins were still plain to see and, wearing trousers to match, she wouldn't have looked out of place with the Khmer Rouge.

'She sent a note,' she said finally and handed me a scrap of paper.

I read aloud her fine and spidery script: 'Tell Janice about the tape. And remember what I said about the police. Love, Sylvia Buckham.'

Janice was quickly on the phone to associates unknown.

'Kim Stove?' Janice mused aloud after her brief and mumbled conversation. 'The *Evening Post* did a piece on her a couple of weeks ago. I'm surprised the police haven't pulled her in, what with her connection to Sita Joshi.'

'Connection' was an odd way of describing a lengthy and intimate relationship. Newspeak, I guessed, known only to the initiated.

'She's supposed to be on tour somewhere in Belgium,'

AnnaMaria observed.

Mum's trip to Brussels was suddenly made clear. Mixing business with pleasure had been developed into an art form.

'Well, wherever she is now, she was definitely in Calderton a couple of days ago,' I insisted.

'And the other person?' Janice enquired, scribbling furiously in her notebook.

I shrugged. 'A woman, I think. Dark-haired, broad-shouldered.' I tried to recall more details from the brief view I'd had of the tape.

'And the car?' Janice's pencil flew across paper.

'A Mini, like I explained. Do you know anything about the number plate yet?' I pressed her, sick of answering questions. She was worse than the police. My head was beginning to ache again and I could have done with Laura's ministrations.

'I'm waiting for a call,' Janice mumbled, tapping her mobile phone with the rubber end of her pencil. 'Likewise the phone Sita used,' she added.

AnnaMaria butted in. 'I still think we should call the police.'

Wallis, who'd awoken briefly with Janice's arrival, had taken refuge on AnnaMaria's lap and she murmured slightly at her raised voice. AnnaMaria stroked the little girl's head gently and soon she was fast asleep again.

'No!' Janice and Julia hissed quietly in unison.

For different reasons, they both wanted the police kept at bay, at least for the time being.

Janice's reasoning was easy to see. A scoop like this, she hoped, would secure her future. Vengeance for her aunt's injuries couldn't be ruled out either.

Julia's logic was rather more complex. Not one to put herself out under normal circumstances, she had been cast as Romeo to Sita's Juliet. Saving face and securing Sita's heart were at the forefront of her reckoning. The added bonus of publicity for Rossi and Marple Motors, especially now the bypass seemed to be on ice, was there somewhere too. And finally she didn't want to upset her mother any more than she already had.

AnnaMaria, common sense and pregnancy overcoming any false idea of adventure, wanted to ring the police.

I wanted Anne.

AnnaMaria settled the dispute by tutting and snatching up the phone. 'Let me ring the goddamn police,' she growled.

Janice's phone beeped into life. AnnaMaria paused, mid-dial.

'Yep,' Janice, scribbling busily onto a fresh sheet of paper, said into the mouthpiece. 'You sure?' More scribble. 'Gotcha, cheers. Owe you one.' She closed the phone with a flourish. She should have been on stage.

'Well?' Julia pressed.

Janice grinned. 'We've got a fix on the phone.'

I closed my eyes. I'd fallen into a Dashiel Hammett thriller.

'So tell the police,' AnnaMaria insisted.

The two women roundly ignored her.

'And the Mini is registered to a T. Pekeč. Familiar, anybody?'

Janice's true nature as an interrogator was slowly being revealed.

AnnaMaria looked skywards with a heavy and

despairing sigh. 'Tracey. Oh, Tracey. For God's sake, what are you doing?' she murmured. 'I should have known.' She rubbed her forehead wearily and turned to me. 'Tracey Pekeč. Sapphire to you.'

'Do you know what's she's up to?' I asked a stunned AnnaMaria.

'Don't be ridiculous,' she snapped, gently removing Wallis from her knee. The little girl stirred only slightly before curling up on the settee.

'Well, you know her better than me. More intimately, I mean,' I retaliated.

She covered her face with her hands. I cleared my throat. I'd dug myself a ditch and I was just about to throw myself in headfirst. 'You know, after the concert, at Julia's place.'

Even Janice stopped scribbling and looked up curiously.

AnnaMaria refused to meet my eye.

I blundered on. 'Have I got it wrong?' I ventured.

'Yes,' she said. 'No!' she corrected herself. 'Well, sort of,' she mumbled. 'Not that that's got anything to do with anything. We just shared the futon, had a cuddle. Oh, come on, Letty, you know how it is. We've known each other for years, remember.'

'It happens,' Janice, worldly wise, said with a sigh.

'Shut it, you!' AnnaMaria raged suddenly. 'What the fuck do you know? Go and peddle your fucking lies somewhere else.'

She stormed from the room and crashed into the bathroom, leaving us stunned and open-mouthed. Wallis slept on.

'Not a word, Julia,' I warned.

She shrugged, adopting an innocent and hurt pose.

Janice tapped her teeth with her pencil, a habit that would annoy me, given time. 'I'd go after her if I were you,' she said thoughtfully.

I avoided a hasty, ill-considered reply and followed AnnaMaria into the bathroom. She was taking great gulps of cold air through the open window when I found her.

'Are you okay?' I ventured quietly, not wanting to make a volatile situation worse.

'Not really,' she said in a less than normal tone of voice. She turned to face me. Her eyes were bright with tears and her cheeks flushed with the night air.

'AnnaMaria?' I asked quietly.

'I'm sorry, Letty. I should have told you before.'

'What?' I asked, distressed by her obvious pain.

She buried her face in her hands again, great gulping sobs suddenly breaking through her shaky reserve.

'That night,' she began, but faltered as tears stole her words.

I shuffled over to her and hugged her, rubbing her arm in what I hoped was a comforting way.

After a moment she stopped crying, wiped her face with the back of her hand and sniffed.

'That night,' she tried again. 'At Julia's. Letty, I know you saw us in the club. And I know I tried to dismiss it. But I can't any more. It's just so fucking painful.'

'You know you can tell me,' I urged, though by this time I was beginning to guess anyway.

'We were a lot closer than I let on, you know.'

I nodded and gave her arm another rub.

'She was my first . . .' She faltered and sobbed again.

'My first lover. And I did love her. Oh, I know I was young and all that.'

I didn't want to ask how young.

'But we were the same age, we had the same outlook. Christ, you know she was more of a rebel than even I was. And we had this thing going. I'd have done anything for her. When she left Calderton she promised to keep in touch. But she never did,' she said quietly. 'And I've never forgotten her, you know. Anyway, I started going out with blokes. They're much easier to deal with.'

I was getting a bit more information thrown at me than I really needed by this time.

'I met Andy and I really love him. Or I thought I did. But then Tracey reappeared and it's done my head in seeing her again. It's as though she's never been away.' She paused to look at me. 'And now this. What has she got herself involved in? Letty, I really don't know what to do.'

I didn't have an answer. A thousand questions, but no answers to AnnaMaria's dilemma.

'Well,' I said after a minute. 'Let's see what this is all about first, okay? Let's not jump to any conclusions, shall we? The only person who can help you sort this out is Sapphire – sorry, Tracey.'

As a solution to a problem, that was about the crappiest I'd ever come up with.

'Okay,' AnnaMaria agreed. 'But keep Janice away from me. Bloody vultures, the lot of them.'

'It was my fault as much as anybody's. She'd still be sat in the Metro if it wasn't for me,' I said with a smile.

'It doesn't really matter.' AnnaMaria sighed. 'I suppose I should have told you.'

I took a seat opposite her on a bath that would have dwarfed a rugby team. 'Well, you have now.'

AnnaMaria chewed her bottom lip for a moment before replying.

'There's more, about Tracey. She's got really weird.'

I laughed aloud before I could stop myself. 'Well, she was never exactly normal,' I said for want of a better word.

AnnaMaria was beyond laughter.

'How weird?' I prompted.

'It's hard to explain. That night, after the concert, she never shut up about Sita Joshi. I thought she just liked working for her at first, but there was more to it than that. It was an obsession. I can't really describe it any better. At first I thought I was just being jealous. Crazy, isn't it? But she knew too much about her for an employee. She seemed to know things about her that even a family wouldn't know.'

Great chasms of thought opened up before me, endless possibilities of a fatal attraction that I couldn't help but be curious about.

'Like what?'

'Oh, her past, her friends. Even her relationships. And then that thing with Kim Stove.'

'What thing?' I encouraged, leaning closer.

A bang on the door interrupted our conversation.

'Are you going to be in there all night?' Julia yelled.

There was no reasoning with Julia. The bit was firmly between her teeth and we all had to ride along with her.

'Come on, it'll keep,' AnnaMaria said. 'And thanks, Letty.'

She hugged me.

'It won't go any further, you know.'

'I know,' she said quietly, and smiled a rather sad and lonely smile.

Trundling back into the lounge, I saw Janice hovering near the front door.

'Come on, Julia,' she hissed. 'Let's go.'

But Mrs Rossi, finally leaving her bedroom, stopped her offspring before she had a chance to leave.

'Mama,' Julia sighed after words had been exchanged. Italian was the chosen language of communication. AnnaMaria interpreted the conversation. 'You wouldn't think she was in her forties, would you?' she said in a more usual tone, as Julia desperately tried to handle her mum.

Where the hell do you think you're going?' I demanded of Janice.

Janice, agitated at the delay, ignored my question.

'Julia!' she hissed again.

'Even her mum thinks she should ring the cops,' AnnaMaria whispered.

The conversation got more heated, but in the end a set of keys was thrust into Julia's hands.

'For God's sake,' I yelled at Julia as she made for the door.

'What?' she bellowed back.

Clearly agitated, she had her sights set on a particular course of action and whatever I said, it wasn't going to stop her. I edged in front of the door, blocking her path.

'You can't just leave,' I said.

'Letty! Move!' she ordered.

'It could be dangerous,' I tried.

'Don't be melodramatic. I'm going after Sita. And

that's all there is to it. Now please, just step aside.'

Julia was ghostly pale but determined, and I stepped away from the door, realising I was physically unable to stop their departure. The two women brushed past me.

'Be careful,' AnnaMaria muttered, to everybody's amazement.

There was silence for a moment after they'd left, broken only by Mrs Rossi's cry of despair. She slowly strangled her handkerchief.

'Janice, I can understand, but my daughter, she is too old for these –' she paused, reaching for the right word – 'theatricals.'

AnnaMaria raised an eyebrow.

'It is not her nature,' Mrs Rossi decided. 'This is a strange business. And this MP, this Sita Joshi, is just a friend? I suspect not.' She paused again, close to tears, and dabbed her nose with her defeated hanky. 'My daughter never finds it in her heart to confide in me. Does she think I live in the Middle Ages?' She sniffed, another quick dab.

AnnaMaria fidgeted, uncomfortable with Mama Rossi's confession of doubt. Suddenly the older woman straightened, having given herself a mental shake.

'Letty, please. If you could go after them. Julia has taken the hire car. A black Porsche.' Mrs Rossi never did things by half. 'Quickly, before they leave.'

'I'll go,' AnnaMaria offered. 'Letty, you're not up to it.'

'And you are?' I asked, with a smile.

She grinned back, a definite improvement on her mood of moments ago.

'Letty?' Sophia urged.

Mrs Rossi's orders were not to be ignored and I

checked I had the keys to the Volkswagen before I struggled after the two women.

'AnnaMaria,' I heard Sophia say, 'Inspector Davenport, do you have his number?'

Chapter 24

Despite an initial battle between the clutch and my injured ankle, I was soon on Julia's trail.

I needn't have worried about keeping up with them. After following the Porsche on the motorway for an hour, it was obvious they were heading back to Calderton. I barrelled down the M62, dipped headlights keeping the hired car in distant view. The VW engine, unused to the demands I was making on it, roared its protest from under the bonnet.

Madness, the whole thing was madness. I should have been in bed, watching telly and resting my stitched head and swollen ankle. Instead I was a refugee from *Aliens*, Sigourney Weaver saving the world. Not that I looked remotely like the actress. With my present injuries I had more in common with Bela Lugosi in *Return of the Vampire*.

I followed Woodward and Bernstein down the Todmorden slip road. Home was thirty minutes away, twenty at the speed Julia was doing. As I lost her in the distance, I tried to make sense of the latest revelations.

What was going on? Kidnapping? Though there'd been no ransom demand as far as I was aware. Not that the police were saying anyway. But all that money Kim had handed over was shown quite clearly on the tape. That was the only thing that *was* clear. Maybe it was Mrs White in the dining room with the candelabra. It made as much sense.

Where was the clever-dick private eye when you needed her?

We hit Calderton twenty-five minutes later and, racing through the village centre, I caught sight of the road protesters' camp. Laura, convinced the bypass was a lame duck, would claim the charade as a victory no doubt. Though if the plans were ever dusted off, she'd be back like a shot.

I sped past an open-mouthed Sergeant Sam, obviously keeping the peaceful protest as trouble-free as possible. At some point he would have words to say about my blatant disregard for the speed limits. He was hardly in a position to pursue me at the moment. I passed his regulation police bicycle leaning against the village post-box. Well into his fifties, Sam did not number the Tour de France among his specialist subjects.

And the Monaco Grand Prix wasn't mine either, I thought, as I roared out of the village. Julia's Porsche was faintly visible on the horizon. The road she had taken, best described as a track, had two possible conclusions. My farm or old George's next door. To be honest, I wouldn't have put money on either as a destination a couple of hours ago. It was beyond me to speculate why. I followed the track, the moon and my full beam illuminating the way.

The lane that separated our two farms wasn't used much. George had long since given up any pretence at farming. He'd found an easier way to exploit the land. During a car auction of Julia's held on my land some years ago, he'd enjoyed a brief but successful foray into the role of landlord. It was a money-spinner and he'd extended the idea, each summer inviting groups of Americans to enjoy the British way of rustic life. Rusty more like. His farm had all the charm of a disused bordello.

Half-way down the little-used track I came across Julia's car, abandoned on the grass verge. My friend's unexplained absence in these circumstances scared me. Eerie and deserted, in the strange half-light the track was as unfamiliar as a lunar landscape.

Now, as far as I am aware, the Campbell family has no known links with the Shoshone tribe of North American Indians, but even I couldn't fail to notice the trail of footprints leading from the car. Heading neither to the right, where George's property lay, nor straight ahead, where my house sat in darkness, they led instead to AnnaMaria's beloved but rarely visited area of woodland at the far reaches of the farm, before the moors began to encroach.

My previously unknown tribal instincts also ensured that I noticed there were more than two sets of footprints. Silence and a cold darkness engulfed me. A feeling I would never want to get used to. Call me a coward – in fact, call me what you want – but my overwhelming sense of self-preservation had me back in the Volkswagen and in first gear ready for the short trip to my house, safety and a phone. The car had other ideas. It stalled and, having risen above and beyond the call of duty, it died quietly at the roadside. A squeak from the starter motor was her death rattle and life was extinguished when her lights went dim, dimmer and finally went out.

Eventually my eyes adjusted, though my nerve didn't. Beyond, an oasis of light surrounded the abandoned Porsche, its doors open, the interior lights illuminating a five-yard circle around the car.

Leaving the false security of the useless Golf, I edged towards the more powerful car. As I'd feared, the ignition keys were missing. I toyed with the idea of hot-wiring the car, but I'd only ever seen it done in films and, apart from smashing the steering column, I really hadn't the faintest idea how to go about it. That's the trouble with cinema, everything seems so easy. I locked myself out of the house once and I decided I could spring the Yale lock with my credit card. I managed to snap the credit card.

My mind, preparing itself for the worst, was heading for an inane kind of meltdown. Before long I'd be making a shopping list or planning my next holiday. I'd be found days later, wandering around and talking to myself.

Reality, though, was an owl hooting in the dark, a quick life-and-death scuffle in the undergrowth as unknown assailants grappled over an unfortunate victim. But above these familiar sounds were others in the distance. Wheels on gravel and voices in the dark drifted towards me faintly on the breeze.

A crash of metal on wood, again alien to the setting, had me rigid with something beyond fear. I turned longingly towards the dead vehicles behind me and through the open passenger door of the Porsche I spotted an object I'd previously missed. Janice's battered Nikon poked out from beneath the seat. I didn't give myself time to think why Janice would have left this treasured item in the car, nor why I returned to the Porsche to retrieve it, but in some strange way it gave me a feeling of security and, shivering with cold, and for reasons I couldn't name, I followed the tracks and the sounds that echoed hollowly from AnnaMaria's wilderness.

Chapter 25

The woods seemed deeper, bigger, less familiar than they did during the day. A trick of the light, or lack of it, made the trees seem taller, the bushes denser and the wildlife noisier, somehow more ferocious. I kept expecting to bump into David Attenborough.

I tripped a couple of times, sent sprawling by roots and forest debris to land face down on damp mulch-lined trails. Soil was in my hair, under my nails and even in my mouth. Miserable, scared and wet, I realised I was lost and had in fact been wandering in circles for the last ten minutes. I tripped for a third time and Janice's camera went flying. A sudden flash from the dropped Nikon lit up the immediate area.

Blinded for a moment, a negative image of my surroundings was etched on the back of my eyelids. It seemed months ago but was in fact only a matter of days before that Wallis and I had visited this very spot for our early-morning walk. I remembered the little girl had scrupulously cleared up any trace of our visit. 'So the animals will come back,' she'd said seriously. We'd left it as we'd found it, deserted, trackless and seemingly unused.

It was being used now all right.

The strobe-light effect of the camera's flash had worn off and I was left with a clear and vivid picture of Laura's van. Voices emanated from inside the metal cocoon. Another thud echoed beyond the van, followed by heavy footsteps heading my way. I shuffled towards the rear of the vehicle, away from the approaching steps. Self-interest prompted me to slide unnoticed behind the dark recesses of the van's rear wheel. I held my breath and hugged the metal walls. Discomfort forgotten, I peered beneath the van and watched the familiar figure of Gran climb up the short flight of stairs and into its welcoming warmth. Sprightly and fit, hugging a bundle of newly cut branches, she showed no sign of the pneumonia with which she had supposedly been stricken. The door slammed behind her and a key sounded in the lock.

Slowly I got to my feet. My ankle, twisted again by the recent fall, threatened to fold under me. Balancing on my one good foot, I craned my neck for a look through the van's tiny back window.

The voices from inside the vehicle got louder and I recognised at least one. Cultured but shaky, Sita could be heard quite clearly. 'What was that noise?' she asked.

'Nothing,' Gran replied. 'You're hearing things.'

Sita, Gran. Who else was in there? And where were Julia and Janice?

Straining, I managed a quick glance through the half-curtained window. They were all there. Sita, very much alive, sat erect in one corner, with Julia sprawled at her feet. Janice, pale-faced and dark-eyed, stood behind her. Laura was opposite them, peering intently through another window, a shotgun held loosely in one hand.

Shocked and scared all over again, I finally lost my grip. I scrabbled feebly for purchase on the metal walls and my dirt-encrusted nails made their own unpleasant tune against the painted panels as I slid to the floor.

'Now I did hear that,' Sita murmured nervously.

I began to crawl away. I didn't know what the hell was going on and I didn't want to find out. Whatever Julia's predicament, I was no match for a shotgun. Young men and women dressed in blue got paid twenty grand a year for handling things like that. What was I supposed to do? Throw eggs? And with that thought I tried desperately to get my bearings. I had to find my way to a phone, despite Mrs Buckham's fears, real or imagined. I had to ring the police.

Surprisingly, there was no movement from the van and I managed a quick scramble to the nearest bush and safety.

Or so I imagined. A hefty boot in the ribs drove that thought, and any breath in my lungs, away. This was something else I'd seen on celluloid, but no amount of acting gave any clue as to the absolute blinding pain. My ankle and my stitched head were but a walk in the park compared to this. I was curled into a foetal position, clutching vainly at the ground for protection. Clawing for breath, I caught another blow, lower this time and less powerful, but no less painful. My stomach and my ribs screamed in protest, though not a murmur came from my tightening throat. A rough hand found a sure grip on the back of my neck and, silent still, apart from a rush of air from my body, I was hauled to my feet and frogmarched quickly and frighteningly through the woods.

There was no sound of pursuing footsteps.

We all have fears. Fear of death, fear of cancer, fear of heights, fear of water – you name it. And all the lesser fears of dentists, bad dreams, loss of job. Like most people, I've spent pointless hours worrying over such things. But I'd experienced nothing like this.

Not even a grunt of effort came from my assailant's lips. His very silence was as scary as his actions. I managed a quick glance at his face. His features were vaguely familiar, but I was too terrified to try and place him. His hand tightened on my neck and black spots danced gleefully in front of my eyes as my brain responded to its dwindling blood supply.

Suddenly I was back where I'd started. Mrs Rossi's Porsche was before me, its warm familiarity giving me a glimmer of hope. My attacker, I realised, as he threw me effortlessly to the ground, was a man simply doing his job. With his short hair, grey suit, white shirt and plain tie, he could have been a bank clerk, a stranger at a bus stop or the man in front of me at the supermarket. I wouldn't have looked at him twice. He'd beaten me and had taken no pleasure in the act. What scared me most was that he could probably take my life with as much dispassion.

And then he walked away.

After the first few moments, when I'd hardly dared move, I began to assess the damage. That sounds a bit odd, as though I was checking why the washer was on the fritz or the freezer would no longer freeze, but it was the only way I could function. My tears had stopped and my brain was on the gallop. I tested each limb as I lay alone on the damp ground. My ankle was a fire mind over matter could not put out and I knew without touching my head that my stitches had burst open. Despite the violence, my other injuries were not permanent. My ribs and my stomach were massively bruised but would mend. Provided I was given the opportunity.

I managed to role onto my side, biting my lip to stop myself crying out. From my vantage point I could see beyond the Porsche and the abandoned Golf to other cars parked along the grass verge. The all-too-familiar Mini was there. Black and stark, its engine running, a figure was seated in the front. My suited assailant was standing by another car, his eyes locked on me. My brief fantasy of running away, or hobbling away at any rate, was dashed by his unwavering stare.

The driver's door of the Mini swung decisively open and Sapphire stepped out. Only then did I realise who my assailant had been. He was Sapphire's colleague at that long-ago day out in Manchester. My efforts to make any more sense of the circumstances I found myself in were swept away. A tidal wave of bad omens hit me as she headed in my direction.

Her breath hanging in the chill night air, she stared down at my terrified form. I'd managed to flop onto my back, but that was as far as I was going. Physically and emotionally exhausted and confused, I had to let Sapphire make the next move.

Chapter 26

'Sorry about that,' she said calmly.

She ran her hands down my body, the strangest and most terrifying thing anyone has ever done to me. She squeezed my ankle until I gasped. Was she going to torture me? 'Why?' seemed a reasonable question.

'Who knows you're here?' she asked.

'Everybody,' I squeaked.

I winced and my innards melted with fear as she grabbed my collar and hauled me into a sitting position. The world disappeared to a pinpoint. A slap across the face brought me round.

I coughed. 'What . . .' I began. Tears sprang to my eyes, throwing Sapphire's still-beautiful features into soft focus. 'What's going on?' I managed at last.

She smiled and gazed into the direction of the woods. 'Money,' she said coldly. 'Power, revenge. Even love. Take your pick.'

She stood up. Dark-suited, her long hair fell freely down the back of her tailored jacket. She reached into her inside pocket and a gun appeared in her hand.

My mouth went tight and dry and my tongue became some useless flapping thing between my teeth. She was going to kill me and I had no idea why.

'Come on,' she ordered and, clutching my jacket again, she dragged me over to Mrs Rossi's Porsche, where she bundled me into the front passenger seat. She went round the back of the car and slid effortlessly behind the wheel. Carefully she put the gun, a shiny short-muzzled piece, onto the dashboard.

'You really want to know why?' It was a genuine question and not simply a menacing retort she'd picked up from a gangster movie.

I nodded, unable to speak.

'All right, so you tell me, who's in the van?'

'Sita,' I mouthed. 'Julia, Laura – '

'Yes,' she snapped. 'I know *she's* there.'

I hurried on, not wanting to antagonise her. 'And Janice,' I croaked. 'The photographer.'

'Not AnnaMaria or Wallis?' she asked.

'She told me,' I spluttered in reply before I could stop myself.

Sapphire frowned.

'AnnaMaria,' I went on blabbering. 'About your affair, when you were young.'

The gun was suddenly off the dashboard and in my face. The smell of the oil used to clean it filled my nostrils. I managed to smother a scream.

'Shh,' she said quietly. 'I don't want to hear any more of that.'

Yelling at me would have been a lot less terrifying. I tried to keep focused on her face.

'She's never forgotten you,' I insisted, overcoming fear for just a second.

Her look silenced me.

'I don't want anyone to get hurt,' she said without emotion.

If I hadn't been so petrified, I'd have laughed at that.

'I just want Sita. She's got something of mine.'

'Money?' I ventured through dry lips.

She didn't answer, just stared distractedly through the window. Her attention came back to me and a dim yet revealing light was cast over Sapphire's face. Her jewellery was gone and she looked older, somehow more calculating.

'You know something of Sita's life, don't you?'

'A little,' I whispered. 'Only what I've read.'

She paused and caressed the gun's barrel. My terror reached new heights. Smiling, she put it back on the dashboard.

'We met in Australia,' she said in a strange conversational tone, peculiar in the circumstances.

I struggled with words to describe her, as if words mattered by now. She was so cold, so detached from her surroundings, that I felt I was as good as dead.

'I met Laura there too.' Her next words chilled me. 'I should have killed her when I had the chance.'

My eyes flickered longingly towards the dashboard and the gun that nestled there. The words 'last resort' kept springing to mind.

She grabbed my arm and gave me a little shake to make sure I was still with her. Bolts of pain ran across my body. I was with her every step of the way. Her dark eyes raged with anger and some bitter memory that she felt compelled to share. I wanted to be anywhere but here and I was more and more fearful for my life.

'I'm sure you know about the women's centre Sita set up in the outback. You should do. She was famous for it. I worked for her, you know. I skivvied for her for years. She knew how I felt about her, you see.'

I didn't see anything. Her rantings meant nothing to me.

'Sita Joshi took advantage of me.' Sapphire grimaced at the memory. 'She used me,' she whispered.

'But you still work for her,' I said, a faint light beginning to dawn.

'No, no,' she laughed. '*She* works for *me* now. How much of this do you need to know?' she asked, almost conversationally.

As far as I was concerned, she could prattle on all night. The longer she talked, the longer I lived. '

'Perhaps I can help.'

She roared with laughter at that.

'No, only Sita can help me now.' She paused and then decided to tell me her tale. 'I'd been in Australia only a short while, and then I met Sita. She offered me a job at the women's adventure centre, and I took it and grafted for her for sod all just to be near her. My God, I loved the woman more than anything, anybody I'd ever met. Have you ever felt like that? And just once she came to me,' she added quietly. 'You don't forget a night like that. It just leaves you wanting more. And then Kim Stove. I knew I'd lost her then.' Sapphire stared back at these distant memories and I could see that to her they had occurred only yesterday.

'So what happened?' I croaked. Was this the 'playing

for time' I'd seen in countless movies?

Sapphire's attention came back to me. 'A climbing accident happened. Only it wasn't an accident. It was negligence that killed Laura's girlfriend. And who was it easiest to blame? The organiser. Me.' She shook her head as she summoned up her thoughts. 'Laura wanted to sue me. Christ, she'd have been happy to see me on manslaughter charges. But Sita knew it would finish the centre. She was controversial enough even then, but this sort of trouble would end it for good.'

'But you said it was negligence,' I managed.

'Oh, it was. Cutting corners to save a few dollars here and there. Buying knocked-off gear on the cheap. Have you ever climbed?' she asked suddenly.

I shook my head.

'It's not something you want to take risks with, believe me. I could probably have proved what was going on too, if I'd been around long enough. But I was out, paid off, sent packing.' Sapphire spat the words out. 'And what power did I have? Who would have listened to me? Nobody. Not the law, not the papers. Who was I? Some foreign little dyke who didn't know anything. And what really fucked me off was Laura and the blame she tried to dump on me. Did she think I'd planned what happened? She wouldn't listen to me and she didn't believe a word I said.'

I didn't bother pointing out that the woman had not only lost her lover but had the responsibility of a baby as well. It seemed to me she had enough on her mind.

Sapphire went on, her tone getting more bitter with every word. 'Sita helped Laura financially as well. That fucking van, who do you think bought that?' she added, a sudden hysterical note in her voice.

'Sapphire, please,' I wailed, almost hysterical with fear myself.

'I knew that the safety regulations weren't being followed. If it got out, well, something like this would finish her.' She paused and the gun on the dashboard loomed large in my sights. 'Laura was devastated. We all were. But she believed Sita. My God, do you know how young I was then?'

It was beyond me to reply.

'Sita thought I wouldn't do anything, thought I was too young or stupid. I could have ended her career,' she added bitterly, shaking her head as though she regretted that she hadn't.

'But the money,' I interrupted, curiosity overcoming fear.

Sapphire smiled. 'Blackmail,' she said. 'The best revenge. I caught up with her in England. It's been so easy.' Sapphire suddenly laughed. 'I told her I had evidence that would put her behind bars. Of course I haven't. But she wasn't to know that.'

Sapphire shook me again and my teeth crashed together painfully.

'You know what I'm talking about, don't you? Her career was the least of her worries. The final persuasion came when I blew her car up. It's surprising how vulnerable a person can be made to feel.' She paused, then added drily, 'I suppose she knew I meant business. And then when her money ran out, Kim Stove stepped in.'

'And Laura?' I asked quietly, shivering with the knowledge that I might be taking this information with me to the grave. 'Why would she believe Sita over you?'

Sapphire shrugged. 'Who knows,' she said. 'Loyalty? She'd been convinced that her girlfriend's death was my fault. I'd been the last to see her alive, and Laura was a good friend of Sita's. Why would she doubt her word? I was only hired help, remember. It was just too easy to blame me. I don't care any more,' she added angrily, her dark eyes hooded and unreadable. 'Sita's got another payment of mine and I want it, and I want her back.'

If I had any doubts that Sapphire had lost it, this last confession swept them away. Her hand skittered across the dashboard and momentarily fondled the gun. Wearily I realised that the attack on me and Mrs Buckham had been orchestrated by Sapphire. Her hands were too horribly familiar. Despite my sense of self-preservation, I wanted to know why.

'The tape of course,' she said flatly. 'Why do you think? Did the old woman think I was blind? It was obvious me and Kim were being filmed. She didn't even have the sense to turn the goddamn bedroom lights off. That sort of evidence I could do without. I didn't realise anyone would be in the shop. The whole village seemed to be at the road protest. Laura sticking her nose in again,' she growled. 'Anyway, it was your own fault for being in the way.' Angrily she shook me again. I managed not to cry out. 'I couldn't believe Kim's fucking nerve. She told me that Sita was somewhere I couldn't reach her and that that would be the last payment. No fucking chance!'

Of course, finding out what she'd done, or even why she'd done it, didn't help my predicament. In fact, it only added to my feelings of doom. The car windows had steamed up with my short, scared breaths and Sapphire's chit-chat. She reached across me to wipe them clean with her long, lean hand. I winced in anticipation of a slap or a punch and she smiled at my reaction. As contender for wimp of the week, I was about to win the trophy. And then for a stunned moment I dared hope again.

Across my line of vision, against the backdrop of trees and bushes, was a sight to set my heart racing. Calderton's one and only police van and Sergeant Sam's pushbike were parked twenty yards away. Even as I watched, Sapphire's colleague was being shoved unceremoniously into the back of the van.

Far from panicking, Sapphire simply laughed and retrieved the gun from the dash.

'Well, let's see just how valuable you are,' she muttered and, with a strong arm around my neck, she kicked open the passenger door and bundled me out of the car.

I hit the cold, hard ground with a bone-jarring thud and I was aware of every bruise, every muscle and every limb of my body.

Sapphire, landing in a loose squatting position behind me, wrapped an arm around my neck and pressed the muzzle of the gun painfully into my cheek.

'Not a word,' she hissed.

Suddenly an arc lamp flooded the area with light. Sam must have made a late-night raid on the local hardware store to get that. We were huddled by the side of the Porsche, unable to see past the dazzling floodlight. A calculated and calm voice sounded over a bullhorn.

'Drop your gun and put your hands above your head,' Sam ordered.

Was that the best they could do? Were they really still using lines from *Gunfight at the OK Corral*?

Sapphire's response was to hug me closer to her. I could feel the trip-trip beat of her heart against my back. If mine went any faster it would go into reverse.

'Put the light out or she's dead.'

Sapphire had obviously had a part in the film too. There was a standoff for a moment, but when Sapphire fired a warning shot into the air, temporarily deafening me, Sam complied and the light went out.

This wasn't like *Cracker* or *Prime Suspect*. On telly a negotiator turns up and everyone gets cosy and clever. This was proving to be more of a 'Cagney' than a 'Lacey' situation.

'Come on,' Sapphire said conversationally, and she hauled me to my feet.

The barrel of her pistol moved from my cheek to beneath my chin, forcing my head up and my neck to a straining point that made me gasp in pain.

'Only do what I say,' she said in the same tone Wallace would use to ask Gromit for a cup of tea.

My eyes adjusted to the new angle and, though I could see only the tree tops, it was easy to imagine where we were headed. Sapphire, with strength I could never possess, marched me from the grass verge and into the woods' protective arms. She loosened the pressure on my chin as the foliage closed around us.

'Let's go for a walk,' she whispered in the dark and, grabbing my collar, dragged me deeper into the damp and moonlit woods.

Unlike me, she had no problem with her sense of direction and within minutes we were outside Laura's van. In the distance I could hear the crunch of gravel under feet as Calderton's tiny police force tried to keep us safely in sight.

Radios echoed over the night sounds. Orders going backwards and forwards to other police not yet on the scene.

I didn't know how much more of this I could take. Bruised, battered and bleeding, the only thing I still had any control over was my bladder, and that was touch and go.

Sapphire dropped her conversational tone when faced with the metal walls of Laura's mobile home.

'Open the fucking doors,' she bellowed and followed this request with a bullet, shattering a side window.

My bladder got heavier.

There was silence from within the van. I was already favouring my good leg when the other threatened to give up completely. Sapphire adjusted her grip and hauled me up onto tiptoe, her left arm clutching me tightly and painfully just below my breasts. Air whistled through her gritted teeth.

'The door,' she screamed again.

Another shot broke the silence and any wildlife still brave enough to be in the vicinity broke ranks and scarpered.

'Dear God,' I managed as the sound faded.

Furious, Sapphire spun me round and slammed me against the van wall. Pressing the gun against my forehead, she yelled a warning to enemies she couldn't see.

At that point I would have paid a fortune just to be able to faint. Isn't that what heroines, or at least battered heroines, do at this point? No such luck. My adrenalin was keeping me going, that and my ankle, which was too agonising to ignore.

The door to the van suddenly creaked open and a dim yellow light lit up the steps. With one last look back, Sapphire quickly pushed me up the stairs and scrambled in after me.

Laura and Sita sat quietly in a corner, the shotgun, an old Purdey, I could see now, resting across Laura's knees. The gun was unusual and somehow familiar. George, my neighbour, had one. And unless I was very much mistaken, it was the same one Laura was nursing. Why would she have George's gun? I now had another reason to be conscious: curiosity.

I glanced around the van. There was no sign of Gran or Janice. Julia was pale and speechless by Sita's side.

Sapphire, holding me between herself and the three women, backed me into a corner. She sat down heavily on the mobile home's upholstered seats and dragged me onto her knee. A cosy scene under normal circumstances, though a gun in the face is the equivalent of a bucket of cold water.

'Where are the others?' Sapphire asked quietly, a question I would have liked to ask.

Laura looked surprised. I'd obviously blabbed some information she would have preferred to keep to herself.

'They've gone for the police,' she said calmly.

'They're outside,' I squeaked, suddenly brave.

Sapphire's arm tightened around my neck. No more squeaks from me.

Someone began to sob. Me again. I tried to control myself.

Laura held up a hand and smiled at me. 'It's okay,' she murmured.

Immediately I felt protected by her calm and accented voice. That ability to heal a physical ailment was being used to reassure my sorely tried mind.

Astonishingly, my terror was swept away. Even the pain diminished and I was objective again, almost detached from my surroundings. I was left with only a distant awareness of Sapphire's dangerous presence.

'Is there any point to this?' Laura asked her quietly.

The words hung in the air as Sapphire tensed beneath me.

'You fucked with me too often,' she growled.

Her words made no sense, but by then nothing did. Her gun came up, but not before Laura had levelled both barrels of the Purdey at her. Immediately the pistol was turned back to me. If it hadn't been so scary, it would have been hilarious. But I knew what George's gun was capable of. There had been no trace left of the last rat he'd blasted.

Sita, silent until now, was wide-eyed with shock. But still her voice was steady and her manner calm.

'Sapphire, it is over. We must both face whatever we have to. The police will not allow this thing to happen. I will not allow it to happen. We are not animals. Sapphire, you must not harm this woman. Such violence helps no one.'

Sita's tone was compelling, her words sure and reasonable. But reason was not in Sapphire's vocabulary and her gun ground my cheek painfully against my teeth.

'You, I'll take you instead,' she said to the woman she'd spent much of her life tearing her heart over.

The politician got to her feet, a grand and proud gesture. There was a moment before she spoke.

'It should not have come to this, Sapphire. We should have dealt with this a long, long time ago. But, if you wish, take me instead and let this woman go. You have done her enough injustice.'

'Injustice?' Sapphire said incredulously. 'You talk to me of injustice? Have you any idea how I felt about you? I would have done anything – '

'Sapphire!' Sita's voice rose commandingly. 'Of course I knew of your feelings. I am not a fool.' She paused. 'But perhaps that is a lie. It was foolishness, foolishness and pity, that persuaded me to let you stay on at the centre, and stupidity that allowed me to let this continue.' She paused and steadily held Sapphire's gaze. 'Only shame stopped me going to the police. Sapphire, you must realise now that it is finished. We must stop this while we can.'

With oratory like that she can rely on my vote at the next election. Sapphire, though, had other ideas. Her breath was coming in short gasps and, despite Laura's influence, I felt fear come roaring back.

'I can't stop this,' Sapphire screamed and pointed the unwavering weapon at Sita.

To say that I didn't feel some degree of relief that Sapphire's attention was directed anywhere else would have been a lie. But somehow it was wrong. This shit had gone on long enough. Laura's strange psychic energy picked up these thoughts. Perhaps a tightening of the shoulders or the clenching of my jaw was the outward sign of my intentions. Whatever it was, we moved together, as in tune as any synchronised swimmers. Sita took a step forward, to offer herself in my place, and Sapphire's gun followed her every move.

That long-fingered hand that had been used so cruelly in my company offered itself to a gesture I could not resist. My body was fucked, my mind in a mess, but one thing still worked. The last thing to give up the ghost would be my mouth and that thumb presented too tempting a target. My teeth, strong, white and good for a few more years, found their target. Of course, biting a gunman can only ever be a stop gap measure. I hoped Laura was ready, because I knew if I got this wrong Sapphire would rip my head off.

With her mind already on taking Sita hostage, Sapphire's grip on my neck had eased, giving me my chance to lurch forward.

Several things happened at that moment.

As my teeth sank into the soft base of Sapphire's hand, the door to the van was suddenly flung open and AnnaMaria came tearing into the room. Julia, launching herself like a blue-skirted prop forward, lunged at the young woman, hitting her somewhere just above the knees.

'Tracey!' AnnaMaria yelled, as Julia thundered into her.

Sapphire's gun went off, loud and terrifying, but for long frozen moments after that there was only silence.

Chapter 27

'Ow, ow, ow,' Julia muttered. On and on she went, breaking the strange lull.

I could taste blood in my mouth. Not my own either, and that was a fairly disgusting thought.

The gun had gone spinning from Sapphire's hand, but she'd still managed to land a few punches with her left arm as we wrestled each other to the floor. But my teeth had remained embedded in her hand until Laura's shotgun, black and menacing, had driven any thoughts of further resistance from Sapphire's mind.

'Ow, ow OW!' Julia's cries became more insistent.

I fell to the floor and crawled over to the jumble of bodies near the doorway.

'AnnaMaria,' I managed.

'Never mind her. What about me?' Julia moaned. 'I've been shot, for God's sake.' And then she burst into tears. 'I want my mother,' she wailed.

'Shut up, Julia,' AnnaMaria said. 'And let me look.'

They disengaged themselves from each other, Julia

sobbing all the while.

The room was in semi-darkness. At some point the light had been smashed.

'It's just a scratch, Julia,' AnnaMaria informed her.

'Are *you* all right, AnnaMaria?' I asked.

'Better than you lot by the looks of things,' she observed shakily.

Sam's gang burst through the door at that point and Emma, his highly desirable constable, stumbled into the room. Sapphire wasn't allowed the luxury of a last few words. Emma's sleight of hand with the cuffs and brisk removal of her prisoner saw to that.

I think I was the only person to see the look that passed between AnnaMaria and Sapphire. It could have meant anything, but AnnaMaria's look of sadness suggested it meant something to her.

Tender hands checked me for serious damage and a grateful and relieved Sita chucked me under the chin before seeing to her sobbing lover.

Lights from a camera could be seen through the open door: Janice, having found the dropped Nikon, pursuing her story to its natural conclusion. She'd finally got her exclusive.

'The ambulance is on its way,' Sam, trying to cope with the confusion, informed me. 'You'll both be all right soon.'

Personally I would have been quite happy in Laura's capable hands, except for my ankle, which she thought was probably broken.

Knowing Julia, she'd want nothing less than a Harley Street doctor on hand.

'I'm bleeding!' she wailed.

'You've been shot. What do you expect?' AnnaMaria informed her.

Julia passed out.

Sounds began to drift in and out. Inspector Davenport's loud and bullying voice could be heard, though Sergeant Sam's was louder. Somewhere at the end of a tunnel there were lots of unanswered questions, but they would keep. Laura's soothing suggestion of sleep and rest was irresistible. The light became a pinpoint in the distance and, as AnnaMaria left Julia in Sita's worried hands, she tucked a warm blanket around my shoulders. My eyelids closed over tired and sore eyes.

Chapter 28

A loud sawing noise woke me. Sapphire, cutting my leg off.

Eyes wide awake, heart thundering, I tried to sit up but couldn't. My neck was in a brace and the only thing that I could move were my eyes. A swift eyes-right in the semi-darkness of the hospital room pinpointed the source of the noise. Julia, arm strapped against her chest, was snoring. Her pink and perfect tongue slapped against the roof of her mouth, disturbing the hospital silence.

A big grey clock stared at me from the opposite wall: 3.30, in the morning I presumed.

My bladder nagged but need for further sleep was a more insistent message and in moments I was back suspended in the land of unreality.

A loud clatter of cups and the biggest, greenest bosom I had ever seen greeted me the following morning.

'How ya' doing, Letty?' a Manchester accent enquired.

'Urgh,' was all I could manage.

'You'll be wanting a brew, then?' the nurse decided.

Expertly she hauled me to a sitting position and plonked a cup of tea in front of me. It was too hot, too sweet and too strong, but it was the best thing I'd ever tasted. After that I was prodded and poked, readings were taken and muttered over and finally I was presented with a plastic potty. It took a while but thoughts of Niagara Falls did the trick.

I got cornflakes for breakfast, except someone made a mistake and I got the cardboard box instead. Exhausted, I slept till lunch.

I had two days of hospital treatment before Julia, who was miffed at not being hauled off to a private room, and I were booted out. In those few hours most of my questions had been answered, though it would be months before the whole story was revealed, and Janice, not surprisingly, would do that. With minimal resistance, she'd agreed to cover the inquiry into Sita's adventure centre, necessitating a trip to Australia. What a difficult decision that must have been.

Sita, co-operating fully with the authorities, returned to Sydney too, probably the best place for her until the furore dies down a bit. It's too soon to speculate about the outcome of the inquiry. So we'll have to see about that.

Julia, building bridges with Sita, followed her as soon as she was well enough, though Mrs Rossi insisted on going too.

'I would like to make my own judgement about this woman,' Sophia had confided in me the day before they flew out.

I'd taken a critical look at myself when I first came out of hospital. I looked as though I'd fought the battle of Bannockburn single-handed. Of the injured parties, Mrs Buckham was looking far the more spritely. The whole village had been on taping duties to replace the films she'd lost. There wasn't a blank TDK tape to be found for miles. Amna, her chum from the cash and carry, had bought her *Gone With the Wind* as a coming-home present. We didn't see Mrs Buckham again for days.

I had a flying visit from Mum, peeved at missing the excitement. She clucked and fussed until we got on each other's nerves, so she went back to Belgium, just in time for Kim Stove's farewell concert.

According to her lawyer, Sapphire, a.k.a. Tracey Pekeč, is claiming temporary diminished responsibility. I couldn't argue with that. She'd sounded as mad as a tick to me and so for the moment she's being held at Her Majesty's Pleasure until they decide what to do with her.

The only person to visit her has been AnnaMaria, and she is keeping silent about the whole thing. I like to think that sooner or later she will feel able to confide in me. So far, the episode has been our little secret, though Anne, knowing her niece better than anyone else, couldn't help but speculate. But my lips are sealed.

One thing AnnaMaria was happy to talk about was Sita's suspicious behaviour.

'Why,' she wanted to know, 'did she keep paying up if she hadn't done anything wrong?'

Julia, draped martyr-like on the sofa, was uncomfortably in the hot seat but felt obliged to give an answer.

'She was always afraid there was an element of truth in it.'

'And is there?'

Julia gestured her reply. Hands open, good shoulder shrugging, it was obvious there was some doubt.

'I don't think it was a deliberate thing. Other people ran the operation for her. I don't think she knew of any scams going on, but ultimately she's accountable. We'll have to see what the inquiry throws up.'

AnnaMaria had to make do with that.

The very best news arrived finally, *finally*, a few days later. Looking tanned, gorgeous and worried, Anne came home.

Our breakdown in communication had been resolved and my lover was back at the farm and beside my sickbed. Half an hour later, she was in it, gently cuddling my sore but happy body.

Now, the biggest shock for me has been with Anne and her sister. It was handbags at dawn for a while. I suppose blood relatives don't have to always hit it off – Mum and I are proof of that. AnnaMaria managed to plug the gap, though. It's surprising what a pregnancy in the family can do. After some debate, Anne finally offered to put them up for a while, at least until AnnaMaria's baby is due. Wallis was thrilled to be staying and she's on permanent chicken duty until I'm fully fit.

AnnaMaria is back in business, and with her boyfriend helping with the hard graft, she's coping quite well in Julia's absence.

Another surprise was Julia's reluctance to crow about her act of bravery. AnnaMaria can't quite believe it's not been mentioned. I advised her to give Julia time.

Laura had to explain Sita's abduction in words of one

syllable. People make life so unnecessarily complicated sometimes. According to Laura, Sita had contacted her when Sapphire's demands had become too much. God knows why she didn't ring the police, events having surely gone on long enough by then. But, as Laura explained, being outed as a dyke hadn't stopped the formidable MP, but any suspicion of cover-ups and corruption probably would. Even Kim had had to go back on the music circuit to get more money. So Laura had faked Sita's abduction, Gran at first looking after her in a disused shed belonging to George, who, amazingly, had first offered his support and eventually the loan of his gun. Their final refuge had been the van.

Julia was caught up in all this, it was obvious, and if she hadn't already been nursing injuries I would have injured her myself.

'How much of this did you know?' I bellowed at her, shortly before Anne returned home. She'd feigned innocence, as only Julia can, but she didn't fool me. But for the time being, revenge could wait.

Anyway, the top and bottom of it is that Sapphire had kept tabs on me and Julia, suspecting we knew where Sita was, and when we tracked her down, well . . . you know the rest, so you don't need me to explain. But if you do think of anything I've missed, you can fax me.

Anne is reluctantly back off to the States. She nearly wouldn't go, but I threatened to become a private detective if she didn't. So she flies out tomorrow.

I got a cryptic card from Julia, in Australia, today. A picture of the Opera House is on the front. She must have scoured Sydney for that. It reads:

Dear Letty
How is Sapphire getting on with the rabies shots?
Love Julia

I'll have to think on that. Anyway, I'll hobble in now. Anne's got the tea on. With Wallis around, I'll have to get in fast while there's still food on the table.

And I want a last long night with Anne. I'm missing her already.

The Women's Press is Britain's leading women's publishing house. Established in 1978, we publish high-quality fiction and non-fiction from outstanding women writers worldwide. Our exciting and diverse list includes literary fiction, detective novels, biography and autobiography, health, women's studies, handbooks, literary criticism, psychology and self-help, the arts, our popular Livewire Books series for young women and the bestselling annual *Women Artists Diary* featuring beautiful colour and black-and-white illustrations from the best in contemporary women's art.

If you would like more information about our books or about our mail order book club, please send an A5 sae for our latest catalogue and complete list to:

The Sales Department
The Women's Press Ltd
34 Great Sutton Street
London EC1V 0DX
Tel: 0171 251 3007
Fax: 0171 608 1938

Penny Sumner, editor
Brought to Book
Murderous Stories from the Literary World

With Mary Wings, Barbara Wilson, Stella Duffy and many more.

Authors wreaking revenge on editors, perfidious plots at award dinners, murders at sales conferences and in writers' groups – in *Brought to Book* top women crime writers expose the lethal reality of the literary world . . .

'Sharply written stories that shift the emphasis away from the macho gun-toting and car chases that plague the genre.' *Gay Scotland*

Crime Fiction £6.99
0 7043 4578 1

Ellen Hart
Wicked Games
A Jane Lawless crime thriller

When Jane Lawless takes a new tenant into her house, she has no idea what lies ahead. Shortly after Elliot Beauman moves in, Jane and her friend Cordelia find themselves drawn inexorably into the Beaumans' lives – and discover a trail of death and destruction in their wake ...

Wicked Games is a dark and compelling crime thriller by one of the most acclaimed, up-and-coming writers in the field.

Praise for Ellen Hart:

'The psychological maze of a Barbara Vine mystery.'
Publishers Weekly

'The mysteries pile up so relentlessly that you'll just have to wait and see who gets caught without a seat in the game of murderous chairs.' *Kirkus Reviews*

'Her style is tight and hypnotic. Her action brisk and riveting.' *Washington Blade*

Crime Fiction £6.99
ISBN 0 7043 4590 0

Alma Fritchley
Chicken Run
A Letty Campbell mystery

'Julia was watching me carefully. "Well?" I said, "What gives?" Before she could answer, the inner sanctum of Steigel Senior's office was revealed and Steigel Senior herself appeared in the doorway. Julia leapt to her feet and in that sudden movement all was revealed. Julia was wonderfully, newly, ecstatically in love, probably truly for the first time in her life, and who could blame her? Steigel Senior was a cool-eyed, blond-haired Lauren Bacall, complete with Dietrich's mystery and Garbo's gorgeous accent . . .'

When Letty Campbell warily agrees to let her land be used for a classic car auction, she has no idea what lies ahead. Why is her gorgeous ex, Julia, really so desperate for the auction to happen? Is the new love of Julia's life as suspicious as she seems? And why does Letty have a horrible feeling that she should never have got involved?

'Hilarious.' *Evening Standard*

'Irrepressibly bouncy.' *Pink Paper*

'A breath of fresh air . . . Alma Fritchley is a talent to watch.' *Crime Time*

Crime Fiction £6.99
ISBN 0 7043 4515 3

Carole laFavor
Along the Journey River
A Renee LaRoche crime novel

When irreplaceable Ojibwa artefacts are stolen from the school
on the Ojibwa Red Earth reservation, the community turns to
Renee LaRoche – a 'two-spirit' whose dreams give her a special
insight into the lives of her people. Her investigations rapidly
reveal a long list of suspects, and then Jed Morriseau, the tribal
chief, is found on the river flats – a bullet in his back.

Before she knows it, Renee is in the midst of a terrifying mystery
which must be resolved even as she struggles to deal with being a
lesbian in a cross-cultural partnership, maintain her relationship,
find time for her daughter, and sustain her commitment to her
community, where she is not always among friends ...

**'Illustrates the injustices of racism, heterosexism, and
environmental degradation while illuminating Indian
spiritual values through the vehicle of a fast-paced
thriller. The dialogue is excellent, the sense of place vivid
and memorable. A fine novel.'** *Lambda Book Report*

'An unique mystery, filled with authenticity.' *Megascene*

'First-rate.' *Washington Blade*

Crime Fiction £6.99
ISBN 0 7043 4521 8

Joan M Drury
Silent Words
A Tyler Jones mystery

Tyler Jones, San Francisco newspaper columnist, is reeling from the
death of her mother and shaken by her mother's dying words –
that there are skeletons in the closet of her family history and that
now is the time to uncover the truth.

Returning to her childhood home is a strange but also poignant
and comforting experience as Tyler renovates the beautiful but
neglected house which she has inherited. Could she – a busy writer
and lesbian feminist activist – adapt to this life for ever? Could the
warm and good-natured people of the town really have something
terrible to hide? As Tyler begins to uncover the truth she discovers
just how far the living will go to protect the secrets of
the dead . . .

**'A cut above the rest . . . will leave readers hungry for
more.'** *Lambda Book Report*

'This book has it all . . . impossible to put down.'
Star Tribune

**'A delight to read . . . captures the reader right up to the
last page.'** *Gay Scotland*

Crime Fiction £6.99
ISBN 0 7043 4522 6

Val McDermid
Booked for Murder
The fifth Lindsay Gordon crime thriller

The freak 'accident' that killed bestselling author Penny Varnavides takes on a more sinister aspect when police discover that her latest unpublished novel featured murder by the same means. Of the handful of people who knew the plot, the prime suspect is wise enough to call in her old friend, journalist Lindsay Gordon, to uncover the truth that lies behind the seething rivalries and desperate power games that infect the publishing world . . .

'**Has the reader gripped from the first page . . . both moody and hilarious and thoroughly unpredictable.**' *Tribune*

'**The writing is tough and colourful, the scene setting excellent.**' *Times Literary Supplement*

Crime Fiction £5.99
ISBN 0 7043 4595 1